To Tame the Lyon

The Lyon's Den Connected World

Sky Purington

ARE YOU SIGNED UP FOR DRAGONBLADE'S BLOG?

You'll get the latest news and information on exclusive giveaways, exclusive excerpts, coming releases, sales, free books, cover reveals and more.

Check out our complete list of authors, too!

No spam, no junk. That's a promise!

Sign Up Here

Dearest Reader;

Thank you for your support of a small press. At Dragonblade Publishing, we strive to bring you the highest quality Historical Romance from the some of the best authors in the business. Without your support, there is no 'us', so we sincerely hope you adore these stories and find some new favorite authors along the way.

Happy Reading!

CEO,   Dragonblade   Publishing

Additional Dragonblade books by Author Sky Purington

Highlander's Pact Series

The Lyon's Den Connected World

Other Lyon's Den Books

Table of Contents

About the Book

Can a woman and her daughter heal the broken heart of a grieving man? Or will ghosts of old keep him forever distanced?

When her rake of a husband promises her to another before he dies, Clara Ainsworth, Duchess of Surrey, has no choice but to seek out matchmaker Mrs. Dove-Lyon and the protection of another marriage. More so, she must trick her childhood love, Isaac, into a union, not just for her sake, but his. At one time, he had been there for her, so she's determined to return the favor and see him free of his self-destructive ways.

Having suffered more loss than most, Isaac MacLauchlin, Marquess of Durham, frequents the Lyon's Den to drown his grief in liquor. Or so he leads others to believe. In truth, he's keeping tabs on his lost love, Clara. So imagine his surprise when she tricks him into a marriage contract to avoid the results of a pre-duel agreement. Naturally, he will protect her, but marrying her is another story. It might come at too high a risk to his wounded heart.

Will Isaac and Clara be able to find their way back to each other and deal with the madman who might be on his way? Find out as the past merges with the present in a tale of regret, forgiveness, and new beginnings.

Prologue

Northern England, 1796

"Clara," her mother would warn. *"Go no further, my sweet dear. You are too young to wander about a strange place alone."*

Yet wander she did, drawn deeper into the recesses of the splendid castle with all its regal people staring down from their gilded-framed paintings. Some English, some Scottish, all wondered what she would do next. How daring she really was.

"I believe you know what I am up to," she whispered, responding to their curiosity. "I have come to play for you, if only…"

Was there a pianoforte here? Dare she hope?

Compelled, she drifted further into the abyss, past grand rooms that allowed her but a moment of escape from the loss of her mother. She should turn back. Her father would be furious. But she could not help herself.

Just a few more steps.

Just to see if she would come across the right room.

"And what will happen if you do?" she imagined the friendliest of pictures asking. A rosy-cheeked woman in ancient clothing. *"They will hear you if you play."*

She was just about to pass another room but stopped short.

There it was.

A stunning pianoforte made of gleaming mahogany and pristine ivory keys.

Needing its sanctuary, she drifted that way and sat. Dare she touch it? Was she that brave?

"Well, you have come this far," a miserly fellow from another portrait pointed out. *"You might as well go all the way."*

He was absolutely right.

So, she pressed down tentatively on one of its magnificent keys.

"Perfectly in tune," she murmured, reeled in by the sound. Utterly enchanted.

Not giving it another thought, she placed her fingers on the keys, closed her eyes, and chased the next note. Then the next and the next until the music flowed, and she said goodbye to her mother the only way she knew how.

On the sweet soulful melody she played.

It felt like coming home and leaving all at once. Like embracing her mother while letting her go. Tears fell, but she did not care. Instead, she gave herself over to them, lulled into a much-needed sense of peace, until the very last note echoed off the walls.

"Are you well, my lady?" came a curious voice, pulling her from her reverie. "Should we fetch your father?"

Her eyes snapped open. Startled by the boys who had appeared out of nowhere, she stood abruptly and shook her head.

"My apologies, my lords," she stammered, assuming them fellow nobility based on their clothing.

"Whatever for?" the first boy said, obviously the one in charge. Taller with dark hair and intense blue eyes, he glanced from the pianoforte to her. "You play well."

"Aye, you do," the shorter, blonde-haired one agreed, his accent the same as the other's with just a touch of a Scottish burr. "I'm Andrew MacLauchlin, son to the Marquess of Durham." He gestured at the other boy. "This is my brother, Isaac."

4

She introduced herself, not sure what else to say. All she knew was her father would be most displeased at her predicament. No matter what one's age, one should *not* be unchaperoned with two boys.

"Why are you wandering about on your own?" Isaac glanced from the pianoforte to her, forthright to a fault. "And why do you cry?"

Mortified, she brushed away her tears and shrugged. Though not inclined to answer, something about the way he looked at her made the truth come right out. "Because my mother just died."

Where Andrew offered his condolences and left it at that, Isaac said he was sorry, then focused on what he considered the matter at hand. "What will become of you now, my lady?" He cocked his head, clearly aware that her father currently visited with Lord Durham in his study. "Though I dare say it interesting you remain with your father when you should be educating elsewhere, yes?"

"My mother was unconventional," she explained, "and wished me raised and educated at home."

"Do you imagine that will change now?"

"Most likely," she said softly. Though tempted to cry again, the time for that had passed. She must behave like a lady now. So she stood up straighter and clasped her hands in front of her, sure to appear well-mannered. "Father would prefer it."

"Will leaving your da not make you sad?" Andrew frowned. "Where will you go?"

"Wherever I will get the best education, I suppose."

"Then what?" Isaac asked.

"Then, I will marry."

"Who?"

She shrugged. "Whoever makes a good match, I would think."

Isaac considered that. "Your father is an earl."

"Yes," she confirmed.

"Then I will suggest you educate right here in Durham," Isaac stated, shocking her, "so that we might know each other better and marry someday." He nodded once, as though pleased with his decision. "Very good, then." Done with the discussion, he bowed, then strode for the door, calling over his shoulder, "I look forward to hearing you play my pianoforte again when you are my wife, my lady."

With that, they were gone.

Clara frowned. Well, how very presumptuous. She would marry who she pleased.

It turned out, however, who she pleased eventually proved Isaac's words true, indeed.

More so, they ended up being her saving grace.

Chapter One

London, England, 1815

Clara pulled her shawl tighter around her shoulders, lowered a veil over her face, and stepped out of the carriage onto the bustling street in front of the Lyon's Den. Though a prospering gambling establishment, it was better known in the right circles for its notorious matchmaking services.

Murky coal smoke hung over the city, and gas lanterns cast shadows on scantily dressed women luring men into alleyways. Trotting horse hooves mixed with raucous laughter and the cool air reeked of animal refuse and cheap perfume.

A woman opened a side door for her. "Right this way, my lady."

Clara nodded thank you, understanding she was addressed that way out of discretion lest anyone on the street overhear. She headed down a hallway to what appeared a ladies' dining room, then on to a dimly lit observation gallery overlooking the gaming hall.

"Mrs. Dove-Lyon will be with you shortly," the woman informed her, before she closed the door, leaving Clara alone.

Violin music played softly in the background of a spacious, bustling room below, and a dim haze of cigar smoke hovered around gaming men. Some played most seriously, where others seemed keener on cocktailing and socializing.

"Oh, Isaac," she whispered, finding her childhood friend in no time. How could she not, when he was amongst the tallest and most boisterous of them all?

Also, quite clearly, the most inebriated.

Though it seemed impossible considering the ample carousing he reportedly did, Isaac MacLauchlin, Marquess of Durham, was more handsome than ever with his thick ebony hair and striking blue eyes. His shoulders were even broader than she remembered, and his features more chiseled. Though he sat at a card table declaring this and that to the dealer, his gaze often wandered to the curvaceous women meandering about.

"All a show, my dear," came a soft voice before an attractive older woman melted out of the shadows. "At least when it comes to women." She introduced herself as Mrs. Dove-Lyon.

Her astute gaze never left Clara. "Normally, I would invite you to join me in my private room, Your Grace," her gaze flickered from Isaac back to Clara, "but I think perhaps it is best we discuss things right here."

She nodded, grateful Mrs. Dove-Lyon had the foresight to make this room empty, for surely she had. "You will help me, then?"

"We will help each other," the older woman corrected. "You understand the marquess spends a substantial amount of coin in my establishment." She perked a brow. "That losing his patronage will not come cheap."

"Nor would I expect it to." She flinched when Isaac roared an obscenity at a patron who evidently offended him. "I will pay it, though, for this cannot go on, nor can my daughter and I remain alone."

What she did not say, but Mrs. Dove-Lyon already knew, was the more pressing reason she needed Isaac to become her husband. The extra protection it would afford her given the rumored outcome of a recent duel.

8

"You are still fairly young and quite lovely beneath that veil." Mrs. Dove-Lyon tilted her head. "Why take on such a man when you could have any you please?" Her gaze returned to Isaac. "For, as is evident by his reckless behavior, he's more troubled than most."

She wasn't surprised by the flash of pity in Dove-Lyon's eyes. If Isaac frequented this establishment as much as rumor had it, then surely she'd glimpsed the man beneath and felt sorry for him. What was this about admiring women being a show, though?

"How troubled is he?" Clara asked softly, grateful for the woman's bluntness.

"I cannot speak to the extent other than to say troubled enough." She sighed. "His patronage of late is becoming far too disruptive."

Such information could be used for bargaining power, but Clara wasn't here for that, and Dove-Lyon knew it.

"It saddens me to hear that." Clara's gaze went to the man beside Isaac, who clasped his shoulder and roared with laughter. With wavy wheat-colored hair and classically handsome features, he likely turned a head or two. "Who is that with him?"

"That is my lord's ever-faithful companion in crime." Mrs. Dove-Lyon considered the man. "Though a cousin held in high esteem, I have yet to determine if Blake MacLauchlin, Viscount of Lorne, is friend or foe." She gave Clara a look. "All I know is where Durham goes, Lord MacLauchlin, as he prefers to call himself, follows and has his ear more often than not."

"I will keep that in mind."

"You should." The older woman grew serious, hinting at a soft heart yet again. "I hear you knew Lord Durham in your youth, Duchess Surrey. That you even spent time at his estate. So are you certain this is what you want?"

What she did not say, but Clara saw in her eyes, was, did she want this for her daughter? Unlike most, she had not sent Mabel away. Nor would she. Her daughter would be educated and grow up

9

near her mother. Which also meant, if she went through with this, she would grow up under Isaac's care.

"Yes, this is what I want." Not only because she needed protection but because she owed Isaac. He had been there for her when she needed him, so she would be there for him, too.

Mrs. Dove-Lyon's gaze settled firmly on Clara. "Then let us talk coin."

"Let us," she agreed. "And, of course, strategy. Because it's important Lord Durham understand what he is getting into upfront."

Truth told, she would have preferred to go about this when he was not in his cups, but it seemed that rarely happened nowadays.

"Leave everything to me." Mrs. Dove-Lyon's attention returned to Isaac. "I know just how to go about it." She glanced at Clara. "I will send word when it is finished."

She nodded and handed over a purse that more than compensated for the woman's assistance plus money lost from Isaac's future patronage.

"I wish you the very best, Duchess." Mrs. Dove-Lyon glanced inside the purse before her astute gaze returned to Clara's face. "May you tame Isaac's beasts and find a good life with him."

She nodded, glanced Isaac's way one last time, then made her way out.

"How did it go?" Maude asked the moment Clara climbed back into the hackney that she had rented for discretion. "Will *she* see to things?"

As though just saying the woman's name might lead to scandal.

"Mrs. Dove-Lyon was very cordial." She settled back against the seat. "I will hear from her soon."

"Very good." Maude whipped out her handy fan and peeked out from behind the dingy curtain. "Such a place!" She adjusted her bonnet on her crop of brown curls. "Mark my words, this is going

10

from one scandal right into another. Dare I say, testing the limits of good propriety?"

"Yes, so you have told me." Time and time again.

Maude had gone from being Mabel's wet nurse to her teacher. She was also Clara's dearest friend and, as of late, even her lady's maid. Albeit a dramatic one with an overly fanciful imagination and a tendency toward gossip. Nevertheless, she had been there for Clara during trying times, and Mabel thought highly of her.

Of a similar age to Clara, Maude was considered plain by some and fetching by others. Her fair skin was unblemished, and her cheeks often rosy. Yet her true power, or so Clara had always thought, was in her lively cinnamon-colored eyes and the way they captured one's attention.

"Did you see him?" Maude's fan fluttered faster than a woman of the night batted her lashes at a passing man and reeled him into the alley. "Did you see your troublesome lord? The man you intend to let—"

"Heavens above," she interceded before Maude blurted out an indecency. "Yes, I did."

"Oh, *my*." Maude whipped the curtain mostly shut, one eye still on the wickedness outside. Her cheeks flamed red. "Forgive me, madam. I nearly said something *quite* inappropriate."

"All is forgiven." What else could she say when her friend had a tendency to speak before thinking? "And yes, I saw Lord Durham."

"How did he look?" Maude's eyes rounded. "And did he see you?" She put a hand to her heart. "I can only imagine the look in his eyes if he did. The *utter* shock! After all these years and—"

"And nothing," she cut her off gently. Maude also excelled at rambling. "He did not see me, nor will he until I know if all of this has been successful."

"But of course, it will be." Maude's brows pinched, and she cocked her head. "Or *will* it?" She looked skyward. "Oh, but the things you are asking of this poor unsuspecting man." Her fan stilled, and she went doe-eyed. "But then, at one point, he would have done anything for you, would he not?"

"That is neither here nor there." He may have for the girl from his youth but not necessarily for the widowed woman who might have a madman after her. "What matters is that my lord has all his facts up front before agreeing to this, which Mrs. Dove-Lyon assured me he would."

"Quite right, my dear." Maude nodded, then paused in thought before echoing Clara's guilty conscience. "Though one has to wonder how sober he will be when he signs his name."

Like her, Maude knew of his carousing.

"Not very," she murmured, wishing there was another way. But from what she had seen tonight of Isaac's self-destructive behavior, this was best for them both.

Not just that, but once upon a time, he *had* said he would marry her.

In fact, he had said a great many things before fate took them in different directions. Softly spoken words about a future lost to them. A future stolen when a duke decided he wanted to wed her. Naturally, her father had given her no recourse. Why would he when her late husband outranked Isaac?

She had often wondered since if that marked the first of a long run of unfortunate events for Isaac. Soon after, he and his brother fought in the Napoleonic Wars for a time, and Andrew lost his life. If that were not enough, Isaac's wife died of illness, and his daughter, soon after.

So it was safe to say he had suffered his fair share of loss. Grief, he undoubtedly tried to numb any way he could. Some might say that made Clara's current endeavor all the more deplorable. Even so, she had to think of Mabel and could only hope when all was said and done, Isaac understood.

12

First, though, things needed to go as planned at the Lyon's Den.

Where, as it happened, she heard word from first thing the next morning.

Chapter Two

"Durham?" Blake's voice boomed. "Are you awake, old chap?"

"Hell and damnation, keep your bloody voice down." Isaac winced against the brightness of the dimly lit coach and the God-awful dryness in his mouth. "Should I not be home by now?"

It wasn't that long of a jaunt from the Lyon's Den.

"If you were staying in Mayfair, aye." Mirth lit Blake's barely bloodshot eyes. "It seems, however, altogether different arrangements have been made."

"Pray tell." He cursed the jostling carriage and braced his throbbing head in his hands. "What did I miss? Are we off to a duel?"

It would not be the first time he challenged another with no recollection.

"Only if rumor travels to the Earl of Kent." Blake snorted. "For you did lay the challenge despite him not being there."

"The Earl of Kent?" He frowned, not liking the sound of that.

Despite having no use for Kent in general, the earl had upset him more than usual with his callous actions. Namely, killing a man who had a family to care for.

"We both know why your challenging Kent to a duel is not so far-fetched." Blake grinned and tipped an imaginary hat. "Though I dare say, you got a bit more heated than usual, which naturally piqued my curiosity." He handed over a letter with Dove-Lyon's seal on it. "Until I read this."

His stomach sank. *What had he done?*

"Devil's teeth." He'd seen this kind of letter before. Mrs. Dove-Lyon had reeled a bloke into a marriage pact. "Tell me I did not..."

"Oh, but you *did*, my friend." Blake shook his head, his frown at odds with the continued amusement in his gaze. "And there is nothing I can do to get you out of this one."

God's truth, his cousin had gotten him out of a situation or two, hadn't he?

Dreading its contents but never one to shy away, Isaac read the missive, more troubled by the moment.

"Damnation," he whispered, both astonished and fearful. His heart leapt into his throat. "Clara?"

How drunk had he been? It could be a bit much at times, but never *this* much. And even when well in his cups, it was hard to imagine him going this far.

"Yes." Blake's level gaze remained on Isaac's face. "It seems the Duchess of Surrey has not forgotten you any more than you have forgotten her."

How could he? At one time, she had meant everything to him.

"Why would I have ever signed my name to this?" He scanned the letter again, making sure he had read it right. "Why would I have ever agreed to marry her?"

Isaac couldn't care less about the contract conditions, which included him taking no mistresses or visiting the Lyon's Den for a year. What concerned him was the disclosure Clara had added. He knew Kent had killed her husband in a duel, but not that she'd been the grand prize if he was the victor.

"Should I assume my need to protect her overcame good reason?" That was the only conceivable reason for this. "I can protect her whether we marry or not." Isaac scowled. "Now she's doomed either way!"

"You cannot protect her as well unmarried, and you know it." Blake shrugged a shoulder. "And she is not *doomed*, Durham. If anything, she and her daughter will be safer."

"Bollocks, her daughter, too," he muttered, cursing the whole sordid situation. "What was Clara thinking?" He raked a hand through his hair. "What was *I* thinking?" He white-knuckled the contract, trying like hell to recall the previous night's hazy events. "*Why* did I sign this?"

He must have been drugged because he would *never* see Clara and her daughter suffer the fate of those before them. The curse, he was convinced, lay like a thick, cloying cloud over his head.

"It was quite simple in the end, I'm afraid," Blake enlightened him. "Dove-Lyon challenged you to a game of high-stakes cards, and you lost."

"What did she bet?" He narrowed his eyes. "What did I bet?"

"She bet your continued patronage at her den and a year of free drinking," Blake revealed. "And you, my foxed friend, the entirety of your estate."

"Hell and the Devil confound it," he swore, recognizing the simple genius in it. "That woman has me well figured out."

"She does." Blake raised a phantom glass to Mrs. Dove-Lyon's cleverness. "She knows you have not one but two weaknesses. The first, a quality glass of brandy smuggled in from France. The second, a taste for spying."

Hence him frequenting the Lyon's Den to begin with. And here he had thought himself discreet. He should have known she would put two and two together.

Isaac tucked the letter away. "I prefer the term observing."

"It was spying and nothing less."

Be that as it may, Mrs. Dove-Lyon undoubtedly used such to nudge him over the edge after he lost the bet. Just like that, he was trapped. Rather than turn over the whole of his estate and risk her sharing his prying ways when it came to Clara's late husband, the Duke of Surrey, her contract was as good as signed.

The most notable thing by far in all this, though, was Clara seeking out Isaac's protection. As Blake had said, she hadn't forgotten him. Which likely meant she remembered what they once shared. How much they had cared about each other.

"Surely you did not think Dove-Lyon missed what you have been up to all this time," Blake mused, arching his brows. "Did you think she wouldn't figure out why you frequented the same gaming establishment as Duchess Surrey's husband?" He rapped the ceiling of the carriage, signaling the driver to stop. "Or that you took a keen interest in his every conversation?"

"I suppose it was only a matter of time," Isaac relented.

"Indeed." Rather than wait for the driver to assist them, Blake opened the carriage door when it stopped and wiggled a flask. "You look rather green, my friend. Let's get a spot of fresh air and enjoy a wee nip to make things right again, aye?"

"Aye," he agreed, glad to discover it was whisky from Blake's distillery in Scotland. After a few solid swigs, he got out and winced against the late-day sun, shocked to discover their location. "We are nowhere near bloody Mayfair!"

"No, as you agreed to, we are en route to your estate in the north." Blake winked. "Yet another stipulation made by Dove-Lyon."

"That I go all this way?" he exclaimed. "Without the woman I have been swindled into marrying?" He frowned. "And how is it you remember all of this so clearly? For last I recall, you were equally in your cups."

"I was well on my way but not nearly as far as you." Blake pulled out another flask and drank. "Good thing, considering someone needed to get you out of there once you were riled. Mrs. Dove-Lyon was smart sending you north. Keeps you out of trouble for the time being because God knows you can be disruptive." He rolled his eyes. "It's a wonder she didn't send you on your way long before this." His brow swept up. "Which, might I remind you, would have worked against why you were initially there. After all, how does one spy when they have been booted out?"

"Send me on my way and lose all the money I spend in her establishment?" Isaac shook his head. "Unlikely." He waved it off. "Besides, I needed to look the part of a grief-stricken chap drinking his troubles away."

"Well, I'd say you accomplished that," Blake replied dryly, knowing full well most of Isaac's supposed acting had been real. Rather than go on about it, though, he focused on the matter at hand. "Duchess Surrey should not be long behind us. Perhaps a few days."

The idea of seeing Clara again made it hard to think straight. Yet think he must.

"You are sure I challenged Kent to a duel despite his absence?"

"I'm afraid so," Blake confirmed. "Despite him being out of the country seeing to business, I imagine at least one of the many present last night will see he receives the challenge when he returns home."

Too true. London was a gossiping crowd, to be sure.

"Let it be then," he growled, taking another hearty swig. If he was in this now, he might as well be in it. "I might not have liked the late Duke of Surrey, but he deserves retribution for no other reason than his wife and daughter being left alone."

Though sadly, if rumors about Surrey's treatment of her were true, that might not be such a bad thing.

Blake sighed. "Now, the duchess is not just alone but in trouble."

18

"Yes, but only if Kent actually follows through with his ridiculous claim," Isaac grumbled. Such nonsense. Medieval thinking at best. "He does realize we live in the modern era? That women are not chattel to be traded off?"

"Unfortunately, not all would agree," Blake replied. "Regardless, Kent claims to have witnesses who will testify to the Duke of Surrey giving him permission to marry the duchess in the event of his death."

"Whether he did or didn't, she would have had to agree," Isaac countered. "And she did no such thing."

"Which you assume based on her seeking out Mrs. Dove-Lyon and, in turn, you."

"Not assume, for I know her," he bit out, then sighed. "Or at least I once did." He shook his head. "Either way, yes, obviously going to Dove-Lyon confirms Clara does not want to be with Kent. If for no other reason than she would not put her daughter in harm's way like that. Not when Kent's reputation surely precedes him."

By all accounts, he was a rakish boor with a troubled mind.

"Just as Surrey's reputation preceded him," Blake reminded. "Yet they married."

"She had no choice. Her father made the arrangement."

"Now her father is dead."

"And good riddance."

"Therefore, some might claim her husband is in charge of her fate now." Blake gave him a look. "However *late* a husband Surrey is at this point."

"Well, it won't matter soon enough." He motioned to the driver that they would be leaving and got back into the carriage. "Kent will have to go through me to get to her."

"Good to hear you are warming to the arrangement."

"I said no such thing." Though he had and was. How long had he imagined Clara being his wife? "Might I remind you there is a reason I've kept my distance all these years."

Renewed amusement lit Blake's eyes. "Because you were married?"

"Because nothing good would come of it."

"Ah, you can only be referring to the MacLauchlin curse."

"I prefer family curse."

"One that has affected no other MacLauchlin thus far."

"But very well could."

"Yet likely will not." Blake tapped the roof, signaling their readiness to depart. "Granted, things have not been easy, and you have had a run of it, but curses don't exist." He looked at Isaac with sympathy. "I know it isn't easy, but perhaps it best you look at last night's events as a stroke of good luck? Perhaps a sign that you should look to the future rather than dwell in the past?"

"It seems I have no choice," he muttered. Instead of focusing on the demons that haunted him, he kept his gaze squarely on the present. "Do you think Kent will take up the challenge if he gets word of it? Might he travel so far?"

Isaac certainly would if Clara were at stake.

"By the hopeful tone of your voice, I believe the correct response is yes," Blake replied. "I think once Kent returns home, he will certainly travel all this way." He tilted his head in acquiescence. "Honestly, out of anyone you might have challenged to a duel, Kent's arrogance and pride would likely make him travel far indeed."

While Isaac liked the idea to no end, he was not without conscience. "May he not bring it to my doorstep, then." He frowned. "For there's a child to consider now."

The idea of having a little girl about his estate again seemed surreal. Daunting, to say the least. Not because he disliked children,

20

he quite enjoyed them, but because it would be reminiscent of his daughter.

"There *is* a way around Kent coming right to your doorstep." The corner of Blake's mouth curled up. "You *could* take the situation into your own hands."

"I could," he murmured, considering how he wanted to go about things.

Not just when it came to Kent but, most especially, when it came to the woman who had long held his heart.

Chapter Three

"Do you think the Marquess of Durham will like my dress?" Mabel asked yet again. She fluffed the skirts of her yellow muslin dress. "For I *do* so want him to approve."

Mabel had taken news of Clara's upcoming marriage well and seemed eager to start anew. Not so surprising, really, considering the temperament of her late father.

"Rest assured," Clara smiled at her nine-year-old daughter, "he will, my darling." She tucked an auburn curl behind Mabel's ear. "For you are the loveliest little girl in all of England."

"Indeed!" Maude adjusted her bonnet and nodded with approval. "My lord will be most impressed."

"Yes, he will." Clara turned her smile out the window and tried not to clench her hands on her lap. To remain calm. At ease. Unaffected.

But God, she was nervous.

When she'd opened the letter from Mrs. Dove-Lyon days ago, her heart had raced and her hands shaken. Dare she hope? Had she accomplished her goal?

As it turned out, she had.

Clara was to travel to Lord Durham's estate, Hastings Castle, at her earliest convenience and be married soon after.

She had foolishly hoped Isaac might come calling first, or at the very least written her, but all had remained silent. He must be irate, and she didn't blame him. She could only pray he kept his anger away from her daughter when they arrived.

While the Isaac she once knew would never take his anger out on a child, her late husband had shown her what men were capable of. Not just that, but people, in general, were known to act out of character when cornered. Never mind those rumored to be drunken and bitter more often than not.

Yet had Isaac changed so much? Was the boy she once knew not in there somewhere? Those thoughts naturally led to more concerns. What sort of life could she expect with him? For her daughter? Had she acted too hastily?

"All will be well." Maude squeezed Clara's hand, no doubt following her wandering thoughts as she tended to do. Even though she spoke to Mabel about her dress, Clara knew the words were meant for her. "Things will go just splendidly." She opened the curtains wider and rounded her eyes at Mabel. "How could they not living in such a beautiful place? And in a castle no less!"

"It really is a lovely area." Mabel's hazel gaze lit up at the rolling green hills rimmed by lush autumn woodland. "Are we almost there? I do so long to see Lord Durham's estate."

"Almost." Clara pointed north. "Just over that hill."

Not all that far from the Scottish border, she well recalled her first ride here. How odd it had been grieving the loss of her mother while feeling the wonder of visiting such a place for the first time. The myriad of emotions as she held back tears. For under her father's strict scrutiny, such was unacceptable. She only finally gave in and let them go at that pianoforte.

While those tears might be long dried up now, she still felt bittersweet melancholy when they crested the hill overlooking Isaac's sprawling estate. Named for his English ancestors who built it, Hastings Castle was magnificent. Though additions had been made over the years, the original castle still stood, dating back to the

23

early fourteenth century. Regal, its tastefully done add-ons only leant to its old-world grandeur.

"My goodness." Mabel's mouth dropped open. "How utterly enchanting."

"Yes, it is." She held her daughter's hand. "A wonderful place to grow up."

It was, too, with all its nooks, crannies, and plentiful history.

"Goodness gracious." Maude stared at the estate and fanned herself. "What an awful lot of space for one man." She tapped her nail on the window as if counting things off. "So Lord Durham has an abode in Mayfair, an estate here, and yet another residence in Scotland? He is of both the Scottish and English peerages?"

"He is," she confirmed. "I believe his cousin Blake, who prefers to be called Lord MacLauchlin, though his title's of Lorne, oversees the Scottish residence, MacLauchlin Castle."

"Ah, yes, he's *quite* the rake, I hear." Maude covered her mouth and widened her eyes at Mabel before chastising herself. "Heavens *be*." She sat up a little straighter and shook her head. "Shame on me for gossiping."

Mabel's smirk dropped beneath Clara's stern look.

"Shame indeed." Clara bit back her own smirk and looked out the window again, glad for the lightheartedness, no matter how inappropriate.

They turned down a drive lined with towering crimson and orange poplars that eventually gave way to immaculate grounds. Juniper hedgerows oversaw melon-colored honeysuckles and lush thickets of red-berried dog roses that had long shed their pink blooms. How often had she played amongst those flowers and the bountiful gardens beyond the archway? Within the enchanting hedge maze, she hoped still remained there?

24

"Is that *him*?" Maude took in the gentleman standing at the bottom of the stairs awaiting them. Her fan fluttered all the faster. "Is that your Lord Durham?"

"No." Though tall and broad-shouldered like Isaac, it most certainly was not. "That is Lord MacLauchlin."

She swallowed her disappointment that Isaac wasn't here to greet them. But then, in his defense, she had gone about this in a most precarious way.

"Greetings," Blake said with a dashing smile when the footman held their door open, and they stepped out. He introduced himself, his brogue a touch stronger than she recalled Isaac's being. "Welcome to Hastings Castle."

Distant ocean waves echoed on the crisp breeze, and the air smelled of sweet autumn clematis.

"Thank you, Lord MacLauchlin." Clara introduced everyone and asked a question she suspected she already knew the answer to. Especially considering Blake was here. "Has Lord Durham arrived yet?"

"Yes, he will be with you soon enough." Their luggage was seen to as he led them up the wide, spacious stone stairs to the front door. "As you can imagine, he's quite busy with matters of the estate."

Quite busy fuming was more like it.

She thought she caught a glimpse of someone in an upstairs window, but when she looked again, nobody was there.

"Oh, *my*," Mabel whispered when the same stiff-upper-lipped butler with white hair from Clara's childhood opened the front door, and they entered the great hall. Heavens above, how old was Laurence now? And was he still wonderfully jolly beneath his impeccable façade? It was impossible to tell as he took their jackets.

The main foyer was much as she remembered, its spaciousness still breathtaking. A monstrous fireplace with an ornate mantel overlooked a hall replete with large-as-life family portraits and intricately woven tapestries. The furnishings were gleaming mahogany masterpieces, and the vibrant, lush oriental carpets underfoot fit for kings. A massive yet delicate crystal chandelier cast sparkling prisms of fading sunlight around the room.

She glanced down one of two arched corridors going in different directions off the main hall. Was her pianoforte still there? How she longed to lay eyes on it again. To touch its dependable keys. To hear its sweet notes.

When Laurence said something softly to Blake in passing, the viscount's hesitant gaze flickered over her before he nodded. Smiling kindly, he introduced Isaac's head housekeeper, who waited patiently nearby. "If it pleases Your Grace, Mrs. Angus will see Miss Maude and wee Lady Mabel to their bedchambers to ready themselves for dinner."

"It does please me, thank you." Clara smiled at her daughter with reassurance. "Go on now, love. Mrs. Angus will see you well cared for."

"Yes, Mother." Mabel took Maude's hand, and off they went up the grand staircase.

"Join me, Duchess Surrey?" Blake held out the crook of his elbow. "Lord Durham has requested your presence for tea."

Just tea? Somehow, she doubted that. At least when it came to the contents of his cup.

"That would be lovely." A master at false airs, she smiled pleasantly and slipped her arm into Blake's. "It's a wonder you and I never crossed paths as children, Lord MacLauchlin."

"It is," he agreed. "But then I visited Hastings Castle less frequently in my youth. The bulk of my time with Lord Durham was spent in Scotland."

Though tempted to ask him a number of questions, she kept to exchanging pleasantries as he led her to Isaac's study. Having been tirelessly raised to do such, well-mannered conversation came

26

effortlessly despite her growing unease. What would she find on the other side of Isaac's door? How was he handling all this?

Blake opened the door and gestured that she enter. "Your Grace."

"Thank you." Crossing the threshold felt like stepping back in time. The room still smelled of rich pipe smoke, and the supple leather furnishings were still dark and masculine. The only marked difference was the man sitting in front of the fire with his long legs crossed and his countenance heavy.

Rather than stand and bow as befitted her rank, Isaac merely gave her his handsome profile and gestured at the chair beside him. "Come, sit, Duchess, so that we might…catch up on old times."

Warmth curled through her at the sound of his deep voice. While it still rang aristocratic British, the slight burr of the Scots remained. She had always liked that about him. It softened the edges of the man his father was determined to make him.

"It would be a pleasure, my lord." She nodded graciously to Blake before he closed the door, leaving her and Isaac alone.

Her nerves might be strung tight and her palms clammy, but she kept calm and reserved, folding her hands neatly on her lap when she sat.

"Please." Isaac's gaze remained on the fire as he gestured at the tea service between them. "I insist."

Though it might go undetected by most, the vein ticking in his temple and the tightness of his jaw told her just how upset he really was. While tempted to take the lead and explain herself, she knew better. Best to let him address her first, then form her counter-argument around that.

"Thank you, my lord." Usually, a maid would serve her, but obviously, he wanted no interruptions or anyone overhearing. Fortunately, though they had trembled moments before, her hands remained level when she handled the delicate porcelain.

At least until he spoke again and tested her ability to remain unaffected.

"It seems the time for stopping what you have started has passed." His piercing gaze finally turned her way. "Now, we will discuss precisely what I expect from this union."

Chapter Four

Isaac knew he was doomed the moment Clara's sweet, subtle lavender scent wafted over him. Rather, before that, when she stepped out of her carriage into his courtyard.

He had intended to speak with her in the presence of others rather than be alone but changed his mind when he saw her. Now he cursed himself for it. What had he been thinking bringing her up here? Having her so close? And now that she was here, how strong could he be?

Though it seemed impossible, Clara had grown even more beautiful with age. Her long hair might be pulled back, but the curls framing the soft curves of her cheeks and dainty neck were still a mesmerizing swirl of ash, golden and pale blonde. Her thickly lashed, almond-shaped eyes were the same pale sage he always had trouble looking away from, and her delicate features both stunning and familiar in a way he'd missed more than he realized.

While part of him wanted to pull her into his arms the moment she stepped into his study, another part knew doing things as intended was the only way to go. He needed to remain clear-minded and levelheaded.

Moreover, she needed to remain free of his bad luck.

Therefore, things must go just so. No denials or arguments but with set guidelines. Logical, practical, and without pomp. Isaac would not get openly angry with her for forcing him into this nor try to get out of it. He had made an agreement, signed his good name, and would see it through.

"I will marry you to honor my contract with Mrs. Dove-Lyon." He remained stern where he would rather lose himself in eyes too long gone to him. "That is where it ends, though, Your Grace." He shook his head. "You and yours will call my estate home and have my protection, but do not expect things to go any further. Once the year is up, I will see you settled elsewhere, and we shall go on with our lives."

"But of course," Clara replied, her soft, feminine voice like soothing balm on old wounds. On anger simmering just beneath the surface. Frustration, he refused to let her see.

"Thank you, Lord Durham."

While Clara appeared calm, he didn't miss the way she rubbed the pads of her forefinger and thumb together. A trick he had taught her in their youth to temper her nerves. Almost as soon as he thought it, her fingers stilled, and her cheeks flared pink. A tell that she likely remembered his advice.

Now that he had settled what she could expect from their marriage, he meant to speak of less important things but found himself adrift. For there really were no less important topics. Only those that had no place in what he hoped to accomplish here.

Distance.

No chance of getting closer. Of picking up where they left off.

Thankfully, she took the matter out of his hands, remaining in a place free of strife when surely, they were on the very brink of it.

"Your butler, Laurence, looks well." She smiled kindly. "Truly unchanged."

"Yes." He didn't meet her smile but sipped his brandy-laced tea, wishing it was something stronger. "He has been loyal."

"So it seems." She sipped her tea as well. "Mrs. Angus seems lovely."

"She is."

"And the estate looks well-cared for."

"Naturally." Had he detected a tone? As though perhaps he would have let it fall into ill-repair? He meant to leave it alone but could not help himself. "Does that surprise you?"

"No," she said a little too quickly, rubbing her plush lips together. Yet another tell. "Why ever would it?"

Leave it be. Yet, the concern in her eyes spiked irritation. Perhaps they would not keep things so civil after all. Then again, they had never been all that good at pretending with one another.

"Speak your mind, Duchess." He downed his tea and set it aside. "For that is something you were once very good at."

Especially when she told him she was marrying another and turned Isaac away.

She lowered her tea to its plate with admirable steadiness considering her cheeks flamed brighter still. "Just as good as you, if I recall correctly."

Had he detected a hint of sarcasm? Because he thought his request that she not marry another had fallen on deaf ears.

Done with pretenses, he pulled out his flask and poured whisky into a glass. "Why did you do this, Duchess Surrey? Why are you here?"

"I would have thought that clear, Lord Durham." She bowed her head ever-so-slightly when he suspected she would much rather look at him in challenge. "I am beyond my season, and my daughter and I need shelter."

"And safety," he reminded, trying to draw her out. "Let us not forget that."

"And safety," she conceded, not batting a lash. "For that, for all of this, you have my undying thanks…and my apologies."

For what happened in the past or now?

31

"You were clear about your state of duress in the contract I signed." While tempted to light a cigar, he refrained, remembering how much she disliked it. "Can you elaborate?"

"Need I?"

"Yes."

"Lord Kent is ambitious."

"Clearly." He raised his eyebrows. "Pray tell, why?" He gestured at her, willing to sound callous if it meant getting answers. "Yes, you are lovely," absolutely stunning, "but why risk his life over you?"

Having educated himself on Surrey and Kent's years-long rivalry, he already knew but wanted her take on it.

"It never had much to do with me." She sighed and gazed at the fire, seeming to weigh her words before her attention returned to him. "Like us, my late husband and Lord Kent knew each other when young. Unlike us, their parting was done in anger."

"Was ours so free of it, then?" Isaac imagined saying but bit his tongue.

He had been furious. Heartbroken and bitter. To this day, he wanted to yank her onto his lap, wrap his hands into her thick hair, and remind her exactly what she had so ruthlessly thrown away. Show her what she had missed. Because the passion had not faded. It still simmered between them now every bit as it had back then.

"So your late husband and Kent's rivalry was long-standing," he stated, focusing on the here and now. "Which lasted to the bitter end, in a duel over you."

"Yes, evidently after their falling out years ago, Lord Kent was going to ask Father for my hand out of spite, but my late husband smeared his good name before he had a chance." Though she barely breathed, a sure sign she worked hard to keep her emotions under control, Clara went on in a calm, unaffected voice. "Suffice it to say, it all finally came to a head one evening after they'd had too much to drink and crossed paths."

32

"So, you had nothing to do with it?"

"Of course not," she exclaimed. "Why would I want the father of my child to do such a reckless thing? To risk his own life?"

Because he was a swine.

She shook her head. "His actions were irresponsible, to say the least."

"On that, we agree." What sort of man would let an age-old rivalry get in the way of family? In the way of his own life? But he knew. He had learned a great deal about Lord Surrey, not just through hired hands, but in person. "Now Kent claims you are to be his wife?"

"Yes, and not because I gave him that impression nor my approval," she replied calmly when she should be heated, "but if I were to guess, he did it to obtain my late husband's wealth through me. The ultimate payback indeed. He would not only end up with his foe's wife but his money."

He could certainly see the appeal in that for a man like Kent.

"So, just to be clear, you did not witness this duel of theirs nor agree to Kent's stipulations?"

"Absolutely not." She shook her head. "I found nothing endearing about the man the few times we crossed paths."

That did not surprise him. They might have been enemies, but Surrey and Kent were cut from the same cloth.

Isaac should tell her she did the right thing seeking him out. That he would protect her above all others. Yet, he couldn't push the words past his lips just yet. Not when he still harbored old hurt. So he kept his tone curt and acted as most men would when tricked into marriage. "As I'm sure you understand, the way in which you went about things is most distressing."

"And for that, I'm so very sorry," she replied. "I cannot help but hope that in good time you will—"

"I will what?" He set aside his whisky, knowing better than to drink it when she could so easily rattle him. "Change my viewpoint on this? Keep you on after a year?" Did she think he would welcome her with open arms? Forget her callousness years ago? "Do not count on it, for I'm not the faithful sort these days."

"Quite right." Despite her reserved countenance, a touch of the fire he recalled from their youth flashed in her eyes. "Things have changed, to be sure."

"Then my reputation precedes me." A reputation he had cultivated so he could remain close to Surrey. He meant to keep quiet but, yet again, spoke impulsively. "Have I not the right?"

"I would say so." Her shoulders tensed. "As it were, you are a man with your own mind."

"The Duchess Surrey I once knew would have phrased it differently."

"You never knew Duchess Surrey," she corrected. "But Clara." Her heated gaze cut to his face. "And yes, the girl you once knew would have phrased it differently."

It seemed he had struck a nerve. "How so?"

"It matters naught."

"It does."

"Why?"

"Because I'm asking." He should leave this alone and dismiss her until dinner. *He* was the one wronged in all this, *not* her. But no, instead, he taunted. Tempted. Tried to rally forth the girl she once was. "I'm curious why you would seek out such a notorious rake to house you and your daughter? Why you would have *ever* thought that a good idea?"

Clara's jaw tightened, and her hands clenched ever-so-slightly, yet her features remained smooth and serene. He both applauded her well-practiced front and wanted to tear it away. Truly, though, however frustrated he might be with her, he was relieved to see some

34

of the girl he once knew still simmering beneath the surface. The vivacious spirit he had once so enjoyed. He'd feared she might have vanished beneath the weight of decorum and a husband ill-suited to her.

"I sought you out because, all aside, I trust you, Lord Durham," Clara replied, drawing him back to the present. To a life he never dared imagine. One that was now possible.

No, drat it, *not* possible.

"Now that I have seen your estate and those in your employ," she continued, "I believe you are still a good and decent man, despite your reputation."

Ah, so she imagined his carousing had led to negligence.

"Are you sure those things alone make a good and decent man?" He tilted his head, bemused. "For a bad man might just as readily want to keep his estate up and his reputation as an employer in good standing, lest he seek more help down the line."

"Be that as it may," she went on, "that you are here when I know, despite your inebriated state, you could have talked Mrs. Dove-Lyon out of this situation speaks to an admirable nature."

He felt a spark of traitorous hope. While he knew she had kept abreast of the deaths in his family, it almost sounded like she'd kept appraised of more. "Do you know me that well after all these years, then, Duchess Surrey?"

Rather than fall into his trap, she circumvented the question. "I knew the man you once were well enough to take the chance." Evidently finished with the conversation, she stood and nodded goodbye. "Thank you for the tea, Lord Durham. I will see you at dinner."

He nodded once. "Perhaps."

Clara would see him all right, but she need not know that nor dictate his whereabouts. She might have led the charge thus far, but now she was in his territory. He would lay the terms. Decide where this went.

"Nowhere, damn it," he cursed under his breath. "Absolutely *nowhere.*"

Mayhap it would be better to take dinner in his study tonight. Every night for a blasted year if he had to. Anything to keep his distance and make clear there was nothing between them nor would there ever be.

Yet as he sat there staring unseeing at the fire, thinking about their past and where it should have led, he realized he'd forgotten to tell her about tomorrow. He could have his butler relay the message but best he saw to it himself.

Which meant he had no choice but to attend just one dinner, after all.

Chapter Five

"I dare say this is a bit much, is it not?" Clara eyed herself in the full-length mirror. "This is merely dinner, not a ball."

"Merely dinner with your new husband." Maude adjusted a cornet comb of pearl in Clara's hair, muttering about their similar temperamental curls. "Your first dinner in your new home."

Clara straightened the sash on her high-waisted muslin dress, pleased with the way the light green material highlighted her eyes. "He is not my husband yet."

"Nevertheless." Maude laid out matching green pumps. "Thanks to your deceptiveness, he soon will be." She shook her head. "I thought this might be a bad idea, all things considered, but I'm beginning to think otherwise. Such a beautiful estate! You should see the rooms Mabel and I were given. Just stunning." She fussed with Clara's hair again, her thoughts fluttering about. "While I'm honored Lord Durham invited me to dine with you, I remain of the mind it was rude of him not to greet us upon arrival. But then I suppose—"

"You suppose he needed to handle things the way he saw fit, considering he was cornered to begin with." She perked a brow at her friend. "As I told you, he presented better than I feared he would."

If anything, she thought Isaac might be sauced and roaring mad, but he was quite the opposite. Not to say anger was not there, especially toward the end. But it wasn't the anger of someone forced into something against their will. Rather his frustration seemed a smidge more directed at their past if she were not mistaken.

Truth told, her thoughts had gone there, too. How they had left thing years before. What she wished he'd done when she told him she was to marry another. Where they might have been today had things gone differently.

When she wasn't dwelling on the past, she could admit to being overly aware of him. How close he was. So close, she could have reached out and touched him. Perhaps cupped his cheek. Brushed her finger over the sensual cut of his lips. Leaned closer and...

"No doubt Lord Durham presented *just* fine," Maude noted, pulling her from her thoughts, "if your endlessly flushed cheeks are anything to go off of." She draped a delicate pearl necklace around Clara's neck and smirked. "I will be curious to see the two of you together."

"Why is that?" she asked innocently.

"You know full well why." Maude batted her lashes at Clara in the mirror. "To see if he's half as smitten with you as you are with him."

"I am not," she admonished, though she feared she was. Where she thought perhaps her feelings for Isaac would have waned by now, no such thing had happened. Not at all. "And even if I was, it matters naught."

"Ah, yes." Maude clipped pearl earrings on Clara. "Because this is a marriage of convenience in every sense of the word." She looked skyward. "I will believe it when I see it."

She was about to say more when word came dinner would be served soon.

"Then I suppose we must be off." Maude draped a cashmere shawl around Clara's shoulders. "It really was very nice of Lord Durham to include me so that we might all become better

38

acquainted." Her eyes narrowed. "Though I'm not sure becoming more acquainted with Lord MacLauchlin is recommended." One eye narrowed even further. "Does he not strike you a bit of a character? A true rogue, to be sure?"

"Come, my friend." She slipped her shoes on, then linked arms with Maude. "Let us not dally and gossip over speculation."

Time would tell what sort of man Blake was. Thus far, she had little to go off of save Mrs. Dove-Lyon's take on him and the brief time she had spent with him earlier.

Because of the long day of traveling, Mabel had already eaten and gone to sleep. When Clara checked in on her, she rested peacefully. Luckily, she hadn't seemed too disappointed that Isaac had not greeted them earlier nor seen her dress. But then there had been lots to keep her entertained since arriving.

"I suppose I must give Lord Durham credit for that as well," Maude admitted after Clara kissed her daughter on the forehead and closed the door behind her. "He did provide some lovely dolls for our Mabel to play with." She put a hand to her heart. "Do you think them his late daughter's?" She sighed. "What a horrible thing to suffer."

It was. Truly unimaginable.

"Yes, I imagine they are Abigail's belongings." She had followed enough of his life to know his daughter's name. "It was very kind of him to provide them."

And undoubtedly very hard.

How she had wanted to be there for him when she heard news of his daughter's passing. To offer him comfort through such a difficult thing.

As it happened, dinner hadn't been served yet, and they found the men enjoying cocktails in the drawing room. Not just Blake stood upon their arrival, but this time, Isaac as well. She couldn't help but notice how nicely his breeches accentuated his muscular thighs. His tall black Hessian boots added to his substantial height, and his white linen shirt and impeccable cravat contrasted nicely with his dark waistcoat and jacket.

Exercising the manners he had lacked earlier, Isaac introduced himself to Maude and urged them to sit on one of two sofas facing each other in front of the fire. After their drink preferences were established and claret served, the men sat opposite them, and idle conversation commenced. Where Clara and Isaac said very little, Blake and Maude were chatty from the onset.

"So you are not just young Mabel's teacher but Duchess Surrey's maid, Miss Maude?" Blake's brows shot up. "That is quite unorthodox, is it not?"

"Indeed," Maude confirmed. "But it really is for the best given the circumstances." She danced around the truth admirably. "The French maids appointed to Countess Surrey returned to the employment of the duke's good mother, Her Grace the Dowager Surrey."

"I see." Blake smiled kindly. "Well, I'm sure you will be comfortable here."

"I cannot imagine it otherwise." Maude's gaze wandered to the imposing family members staring down from their paintings, and out came her fan. "Though one does get the sense they must be on their best behavior."

A devilish twinkle lit Blake's eyes. The corner of his mouth twitched. "Do they now?"

By *they,* he clearly meant *you.*

"To be sure." Maude fanned herself and eyed the broad-shouldered medieval Scotsman with his plaid and sporran. "One feels positively judged by that one." An equally devilish twinkle lit her eyes when she looked at Blake again. "But then he does seem fit for battle, does he not?"

Good *God,* were they flirting?

Based on the quick flare of amusement in Isaac's eyes, she would say yes.

"Aye, he was a warrior, as were many of our ancestors, lassie." Blake rolled his r's with emphasis, admiring not just the painting, but if Clara were not mistaken, Maude as well. "For our people, Scots and English alike, go all the way back to King Edward III himself." He gestured at their surroundings. "In fact, all this remains in the family thanks to a special jewel connecting us directly to the late monarch."

"Is that right?" Maude cocked her head. "And what happened to this special jewel?"

Blake gestured at the medieval Scotsman. "Some say it was used to buy favor for distant relations, such as him." He issued a roguish grin. "Others claim MacLauchlin pirates got ahold of it to rebuild their clan's castle."

"Oh, *my!*" Maude's fan picked up its pace. "Pirates, you say?" Her curious gaze drifted back to the Scotsman with his piercing countenance. "And why was it that one would need to buy favor?"

"Laird Keenan MacLauchlin ruled during difficult times," Blake revealed. "So it could have been for a number of reasons. Warring clans. English invasions." He shrugged. "Suffice it to say there's every possibility he had no choice but to use it to keep we MacLauchlins safe, lest everything fall to horrid ruin."

"Or," Isaac contributed, offering a much less vivid picture, "the jewel still remains in the family."

"How positively *wonderful* that would be." Maude gazed around as if she might spy it lying about. "Does it then?"

"I'm afraid I cannot say." Nor would he ever, Clara imagined. For it would likely be a national treasure by now. "I can, however, confirm that it did well by the MacLauchlins."

Maude looked skyward. "Praise be."

While some might find it wholly unacceptable that Maude chatted so much, the men didn't seem to mind, and Clara was grateful for it. She needed time to gather her thoughts. To sift through the emotions being back here invoked.

Most pointedly, being around Isaac.

Memories of their time together were no longer fodder for nostalgic rainy days but here and now. Part of the present. All around her. Staring her in the face with every familiar painting.

With the way Isaac made her feel.

It seemed like only yesterday they sat in this very room, envisioning a possible future together. It never occurred to them in their adolescence that something might stand in their way. Why would it? Isaac was a station above her, so her father would surely bless the union.

When she and Isaac's gazes found one another, Clara wondered if he was thinking the same thing. If he recalled their countless conversations on this very sofa. He had sat beside her every chance he got, doing his best to keep a respectable distance. At least for those first few years. As they grew older, his thigh began brushing hers, his proximity daring when they were alone.

"Will you kiss me?" she recalled murmuring under her breath one particular afternoon shortly before she ended up with her late husband.

"Why ask something you already know the answer to, my love?" he had whispered in her ear. His warm breath had fanned her cheek, his promises bold. "For you know, I soon hope to do far more than merely kiss you."

Her cheeks warmed at the thought of what his lips would have felt like. The passion he could have made her feel. How it might have been had he come between her thighs that first time rather than a man who only ever lay with her out of husbandly duty.

"You are blushing quite prettily, my friend," Maude whispered out of the corner of her mouth when the butler announced dinner, and they made their way into the dining room. "Whatever could you be thinking about?"

Rather than acknowledge the insinuation, she nodded thanks when a chair was held out for her. As expected, the ambiance and fare were as tasteful as everything else, the décor especially lavish as befitted the dining area. Gentle harp music drifted in from another room, and priceless china and crystal goblets lent to a lovely place setting.

Some of her favored courses were served, including a scrumptious chestnut soup followed by roasted meat, then vegetables in rich butter sauce. Last but not least, one was given the choice between a savory pie and sweet tarts.

She and Isaac continued to say very little as they ate, content to let Blake and Maude get acquainted. Which, in all truth, was unnecessary. The two were not courting, nor could she imagine given Maude's station, moreover her lack of dowry, she being a match for Isaac's cousin. Nonetheless, Lord MacLauchlin seemed unaffected by decorum and noticeably entertained if not charmed by her friend.

There was always the possibility the two simply tried to ease possible tension between Isaac and Clara. If that were the case, hats off to them for doing an exemplary job. All told, though, even if she and Isaac were inclined to catch up, getting a word in edgewise might have proven impossible.

She could admit at the end of the night that she had enjoyed the whole affair more than anticipated. While Isaac often brooded, lost in thought, he was civil, if not occasionally cordial. She figured he would vanish the moment everyone retired but, surprisingly enough, ended up inviting her for a stroll.

One, it just so happened, that became a walk down memory lane.

Chapter Six

"I trust you enjoyed dinner?" Though Isaac had every intention of steering Clara down one hallway, he ended up leading her down another.

"I did, thank you." She nodded graciously. "It was lovely."

He imagined it was a given that, against his better judgment, he made sure that all her favorite foods were served. Which made him realize just how vulnerable he really was when it came to her. How, despite his best intentions to ignore her presence, he was doing the very opposite.

"Lord MacLauchlin and Miss Maude seemed to get along well," he mentioned, putting off the inevitable.

Telling her of their impending marriage arrangements should not unnerve him, yet it did. Perhaps because she looked so stunning this eve. Or perhaps because he remembered all too well how he had felt about this very subject years ago. How he'd struggled to ask her, only for the opportunity to be ripped away.

"Maude and Lord MacLauchlin did seem to get along," she agreed. "Your cousin is quite amiable."

"As is Miss Maude."

They continued on, and silence settled before she commented on how lovely the moonlight was coming through the endless tall windows.

"Much like that first eve," he said softly, speaking without thinking. Yet, as he often did, he recalled trailing after her when she first arrived here as a young girl. How sad she had been. How lost and alone, adrift in this hall, not intimidated by the great faces staring down but rather commiserating with them.

"You remember it, then?" she said just as softly.

Every vivid detail. "Vaguely."

"How young we were," she murmured, her gaze a little lost. "It almost seems like another life now, does it not?"

A life that should have been theirs.

In truth, they were not all that old, but he tended to agree. Those years seemed but a dream now. Enchanted years untouched by war and death. The man he was now but a shell of the lad he was then.

Or so he had thought before she arrived today.

Now, though still irritated, something had shifted inside him. A flicker of hope he dared not entertain if for no other reason than how quickly it could be taken from him.

"Thank you for the dolls you had sent up to my daughter." A soft smile hovered on Clara's lips. "They made the transition here enjoyable for her."

While he sensed she wanted to ask if they had been Abigail's, she refrained, which he appreciated. He might be entertaining the idea of being more cordial to Clara, but talking about his daughter was not going to happen. Though years had passed, and he had healed some, her untimely death was still difficult to think on, much less talk about. Even so, he saw no reason for her dolls to sit unused. Reasoning his butler clearly foresaw, as the items were already out of storage, waiting to be delivered.

"I'm glad they made her happy." A little replica of her mother at that age, he had watched Mabel get out of the carriage with Clara earlier. "I will see more purchased."

"That is too kind, my lord." She nodded graciously again. "Thank you."

"Isaac," he nearly said. *"That is my name, and you once used it often."*

Of course, he said no such thing because he was long past being Isaac to her. No, they were every inch a marquess and duchess now with histories that disallowed them the fanciful notion of addressing each other as they once did.

Back when he spoke his mind as much as her, apparently.

He had since come to the conclusion there *had* been sarcasm in her voice. Why, though? Why, when he'd told her how he felt about her marrying the Duke of Surrey, would she now think he hadn't said enough? Had he initially been taken aback and crisp rather than overly emotional? Perhaps. But she should have known how strongly he felt, regardless. By the way they talked and their undeniable attraction to each other, he had imagined his life with no other.

In the end, however upset she may have appeared, it turned out she would only stand up to her father so much. More so, when all was said and done, it seemed she agreed with his decision. But then why become a marchioness when one could become a duchess?

"Now that we are alone once again," she stopped, drawing him back to the present with her compassionate gaze, "my deepest condolences on your losses, my lord." She placed her hand on his arm, and her finely arched brows drew together. "I cannot imagine the pain. Your brother was a good man, and…"

When she trailed off, he knew she was sorry about his late wife and daughter, too. It had been clear with every bouquet of condolence flowers sent. While he appreciated the sentiment, he was in no mood. Not when this sober. Probably the soberest he had been in some time, and he could not imagine why.

"Thank you." This was the perfect opportunity to remind her why theirs would be a marriage of convenience. Why pulling her too close could prove detrimental to her and her daughter, considering the deaths in his wake.

Yet instead, he allowed silence to settle as they resumed strolling.

"It's still there," Clara whispered, slowing when they reached the entranceway to the room he had been leading her toward. Her gaze flickered to him. "The very same one?"

"Yes." It was the one thing he had requested never be replaced when he became marquess. "It is the same pianoforte."

Clara's gaze lingered on his face before her attention returned to the instrument. "May I?"

"By all means." He gestured that she enter. "It has been kept well tuned."

"Has it?" she murmured, drifting that way.

He imagined her lost to the past, drawn to the pianoforte as he had been drawn to her years before. Her sadness had spoken to him in a way that made no sense then but certainly did now.

Then there was her music.

Her sweet, enchanting music.

Like nothing he had ever heard even to this day.

"I have not sat at a piano since I last sat at this one." She sank onto the bench and gazed at the keys. "I'm not even sure I remember how to play."

"Why did you not play?" He frowned, confused. "Surely Surrey had a pianoforte."

"I'm afraid not." Her fingers hovered over the keys as if cherishing them. "My lord was not fond of its sound. He found it too trilling, so we did not possess one."

Trilling? Had he been mad? Clearly. "Then he must never have heard you play."

47

"You flatter me." She shook her head. "But no, he never heard me play, for he insisted I not add to the ruckus, even when visiting houses that possessed one."

Surrey really was every bit the fool Isaac had thought him.

When Clara hesitated with her fingers on the keys, he urged her to play.

She did not, though. Instead, her fingers lingered a moment longer before she rested her hands in her lap. "Perhaps tomorrow."

"Yet you have such longing in your eyes."

"Do I?"

"Most assuredly."

When her tentative gaze rose to his face, he realized what she needed. What she was hoping.

"I see," he murmured, and truly did. "You would prefer time alone with your music?"

Not for fear of playing horribly but perhaps to be alone with what had once saved her.

"If you would not mind?" she asked.

"Not at all." He was about to leave, only to realize he'd yet to tell her what he had intended. Oddly, with her sitting where she first sat as a girl and he in the same spot as well, the words came easier. "We will be wed in the morning, so you will want to plan accordingly."

Once upon a time, he had envisioned this moment going entirely different. He would have brought her here, fallen to his knee, told her how much he loved her, and given her his family ring.

Instead, they were different people, and she wanted to be alone.

After she replied she would be ready at the requested time, he left her be. Though determined to put distance between them, he couldn't help but slow in the corridor when she finally played. When the same melancholy notes from that first night floated down the hallway. She was every bit as good. Every bit as talented.

He leaned against the wall and let the music wash over him.

Let it carry him away, as it once had.

Her heart, her very soul, was in every stroke. For a time, when they were young and falling in love, the notes had lightened, but that was absent now. While it saddened him, he could admit the music rather fitting. As it once had for her, it allowed him to grieve those he had lost. A letting go of sorts.

In fact, as he awaited her in the foyer the next morning, it lingered in his mind, perhaps overly so as he pondered if it would always sound so relatable. Though not as all-consuming as it had once been, would his pain ever entirely go away? He supposed in time. Or so they said.

While Clara's music certainly soothed his troubled soul, it also had him tossing and turning all night, drawing him back to their past. To the many times they had spent together. To how he'd felt back then and still did now. It seemed the years between had fallen away in an instant, and his feelings for her were just as strong.

So truly, how would he ever stand it if she died, too?

Which, naturally, made him second guess his contract with Dove-Lyon.

After all, he would much rather smear his good name than risk something happening to Clara. To that end, he had decided he needed more time to figure things out. He could protect her without them marrying. Meanwhile, he would come up with a way out of this. Perhaps it was just a matter of getting Clara to change her mind. To make her see he wasn't the man she once knew, that she would be better off with someone else.

"Good morning, my lord," came a small, polite voice.

He had been so lost in thought staring out the window that he hadn't heard young Mabel approach. But then, much like her mother, she was light on her feet.

"Good morning, Lady Mabel." He bowed, tipped his top hat, and smiled despite himself. "Nice to meet you."

49

She curtsied. "Nice to meet you as well."

Where he thought for sure speaking with her the first time would bring the loss of his daughter to the forefront, it seemed the opposite. Instead, there was an unexpected comfort in it. A lightheartedness to her presence helped drive away some of the shadows.

"Are you settling in well?" he asked.

"Yes, very well." She smiled prettily. "Thank you, my lord."

"Heavens be, there you are, child!" Miss Maude hurried down the stairs and wrung her hands. "You *do* have a way of bamboozling me." Her eyes grew round as saucers. "You were to wait upstairs, yet here I find you wandering about getting into all sorts of mayhem." She curtsied to Isaac. "My apologies, my lord, we have quite the little adventurer here."

"Do not fret, Miss Maude." He spoke without thinking, lying through his teeth so that Clara's daughter didn't get in trouble. "I requested that Laurence get Lady Mabel so that I might say hello and share news."

What news? What was he saying? His tongue had a mind of its own.

"Quite right, my lord." Laurence nodded from his perch by the door, saving him...somewhat. "I think that Lady Mabel would enjoy the festival at the end of the month."

Bloody *hell*, that's right. A festival he most certainly would not be attending. One he had avoided since losing Abigail.

"A festival! *Truly*?" Mabel's eyes lit up. "Will you take me, Lord Durham? I would so *very* much enjoy that."

Clara momentarily snagged his attention when she appeared on the stairs in a light blue dress and matching silk bonnet. She was lovely.

It was on the tip of his tongue to say no to Mabel about the festival, but the hope on her face stopped him. It wasn't all that different than Clara's at one time when she finally started smiling when she began finding happiness again after her mother's death.

"Yes." He nodded, giving Mabel what she wanted as swiftly as he once would have Clara. "When the time comes, we shall all visit the festival together."

Thankfully, it was still two weeks out.

Plenty of time to come up with an excuse not to go.

"A festival?" Miss Maude gushed. "How very exciting!" She switched effortlessly from disciplinarian to chummy comrade as she took Mabel's hand. "Come, we must plan our outfits."

Outfits? For a damn festival? Devil take him, what had he gotten himself into?

He shouldn't have given the girl hope when there was no hope to be had. Now just look at the way Mabel stared up at him. The eagerness in her eyes. The connection she surely anticipated having with him. One he ought to put a stop to now, rather than end up in a position where he let another child down.

Yet he did no such thing.

He did, however, rush Clara out the door before Mabel decided she wanted to come along, too. For if she did, there was a distinct possibility she could affect his last-minute idea.

A perfect one, as it happened, to bide his time with Clara.

Chapter Seven

"Your daughter *does* realize I will not be attending the festival with her despite what I said, right?" Isaac scowled, caught in his own trap based on his confusion. "I fear that perhaps I gave her the wrong impression."

The wrong impression? He had flat out told her they would all go together.

"I'm sure Mabel will understand," Clara lied, not above dishing out a little guilt. "After all, she was used to her late father's absence in all things."

"Did he never take her to a festival?" He frowned. "If not him, then you?"

"No." Like telling him she wanted to be alone to play the pianoforte last night, Clara was more honest than intended. "Lord Surrey could barely tolerate the idea of Mabel living at home, never mind bringing her to a festival." She swallowed hard and bit back remorse. "If I took her, that would have only made life that much more difficult for my daughter and me." Rather than risk seeing judgment in his eyes, she gazed out the window. "So, I suppose you could say, preferring that my daughter not be sent away, I chose my battles."

After a stretch, he finally responded.

"You need not look away, madam," he said softly, surprising her. "I will go to the festival…we will all go."

Though tempted to deny she was looking away, she knew better with Isaac, so merely nodded. "I'm sure she will very much enjoy that…we all will."

She'd caught how he and Laurence had covered for Mabel when she wandered off from Maude, and it warmed her heart. When was the last time her daughter had smiled like that? At a man no less?

"Thank you for last night," she said impulsively, clearing her throat when emotion got the better of her. "That meant a great deal."

There was no need to elaborate. He knew. That pianoforte had once done so much for her. Not nearly as much as Isaac himself, but quite a bit. Playing it again had felt like coming home to an old friend. Its keys soothed, giving her back something she thought lost to her. A sense of freedom only found within its notes.

She hadn't meant to play something so somber, but it seemed suited to the moment. To the years behind her. To the things she wanted to remember and hoped to forget. Perhaps even to the proposal she had once dreamt of. Not one where Isaac briskly told her they would be marrying the next day but one slightly more dashing. Perhaps even romantic.

"*Daydreams*," she nearly muttered to herself but kept quiet. "*Fanciful notions.*"

Proposals aside, she wondered at his curtness. Why he seemed so upset with her. It clearly had less to do with forced marriage and more to do with their past. It made no sense, though, considering he had let her go so easily.

Isaac had initially claimed he didn't want her marrying the duke yet never pursued the matter after that. Moreover, though she thought he would propose several times, he never did. Nor, to the best of her knowledge, did he ever get her father's permission. She could ask why now, better yet, the reason for his frustration, but felt it best to wait and see where things went. As it were, it might be a pointless conversation if he meant to keep her at arm's length over the next year.

More futile still considering how, much to her dismay, they didn't end up marrying right away but had banns posted at Isaac's local parish. Clergy would now announce their upcoming nuptials for three Sundays, allowing time for someone to dispute it if they so chose.

"This was not part of your agreement with Mrs. Dove-Lyon," Clara said the moment they were in the carriage again. She frowned. "You are putting this off."

"I'm doing right by my community," Isaac countered. "And as agreed, they are only being posted here, not at your parish as decorum dictates, so the inevitable will not be slowed when the time comes." He shrugged. "The first Sunday is nearly here, so we only have to wait a little over two weeks."

"While I understand a special license would have taken more time and required the Archbishop of Canterbury's permission," she did her best not to grow too upset, "you could have just as easily got a common license."

He could certainly afford it. They both could.

"Yet," he reminded, "that would not be doing right by my community."

His *community*? Poppycock. "What about Lord Kent?"

"He's out of the country on business, so even if he does dare make trouble, it will not be for some time." Isaac looked at her with reassurance. "Either way, marriage or no, I *will* protect you and your daughter."

"It is marriage that will best protect us, and well you know it." She tucked her hands beneath her jacket and clenched her hands. Was the idea of being married to her so bad? "As I said before, you are stalling."

"Community," he repeated. "Plus, this gives you time to acclimate. To make sure this is really what you want."

"Not want, but *need*, my lord. I'm not here because we are courting, and I long for a future together, but because I fear a madman." She considered him. "Why not inform me of this sooner? I swore when you spoke of it last night, your intention was to marry today."

"Whether it was or wasn't," he replied bluntly, his brooding gaze on the countryside now, "it will happen soon enough."

Though tempted to keep arguing, she let it be for no other reason than his darkening temperament. He was impossible to figure out with his shifting moods. Why lie last night? And why not just say what was on his mind now? Because he clearly had things to say.

On that note, why didn't she do the same? Tell him that perhaps, yes, part of her *was* hoping for a future with him. Not just that, but how to this day, she still wished he had fought harder for her years ago. That he had insisted she marry him instead and stood up to her late father no matter how futile. They might have been children when he first declared he would marry her, but she knew his intentions never changed. Not with how close they had become. How much they had cared for one another.

Yet she held her tongue, unwilling to push things.

Where some might wonder why she kept quiet, they would have had to live in her shoes to truly understand. Asking men for anything, be they her father or husband, was not to be taken lightly. Confronting men was a concept long abandoned until just yesterday, sitting in Isaac's study. Though in truth, little was said, she *had* spoken her mind more freely than she'd done in ages.

That sort of behavior, she had preached to herself later last night, was to be executed in moderation, if at all. Because when all was said and done, she had to put Mabel first, which meant not causing any more strife than she already had. The only thing she intended to stand by at this point was her daughter not being sent away. Everything else could and would be taken with tempered acceptance.

Which meant not arguing about a delayed marriage and leaving her and Isaac's history where it belonged.

Behind them.

Yet for all her determination to set it aside, she couldn't help but wonder if he struggled, too. If he grappled with their past and what might have been. Based on his ever-changing moods, she would like to think yes, but there was no way to be certain. Where years ago, she might have known what he was thinking or feeling, it was hard to tell now. Some things she could decipher, where others were questionable.

Namely, how he glared out the window yet still glanced at her often.

Did he expect her to talk? To somehow lend normalcy to all this? Last night, even this morning, she might have. Now that he had put off their wedding and seemed a simmering beast, she was far less inclined.

It was of no surprise when he stalked off the moment they arrived back at his estate. She paused at the base of the stairs and looked up at his impressive castle. A place that should have been her home right now. What might have been years ago. Back in a time when he would have swept her up like some gallant knight of old and carried her through the front door.

Instead, Mabel burst out the door when Laurence opened it and raced down into her arms, quite departed from decorum. But then the merriness in the butler's eyes told her much might have happened in her absence.

"Hello, darling." Clara crouched and embraced her daughter, fine with the outburst if Laurence was. She pulled back and smiled at Mabel with her rosy cheeks. "How has your afternoon been? You seem very happy."

56

"I *am*, Mother." Mabel pulled Clara toward the gardens. "Just wait until you see what Uncle Blake made for me."

Uncle Blake? Not even a 'my lord,' in there? Angels have mercy. Had a rake ensorcelled her daughter in so little time?

She might have expected a great many things when she passed through the sprawling gardens to the hedge maze, but not what she came upon. Lord MacLauchlin and Maude were covered in trimmings and laughing away.

Only when Mabel declared, "She is here. Mother has arrived!" did they pause their antics and grin at her in greeting.

"Welcome back, Lady MacLauchlin." Blake cocked his head and smirked at Maude, flirting to be sure. "That sounds a tad scandalous coming from me, Lord MacLauchlin, does it not?"

"Quite right." Maude blew a bit of hedge trimming off her nose and batted her lashes at him. "Best to save that unconventional title for your future wife." She considered it, stating what would have been the proper title anyway. "I think it best to go with Marchioness of Durham or Lady Durham if you will."

Blake's smirk blossomed into a smile, his once perfectly combed locks askew in the wind. "Makes more sense, indeed."

Maude's grin widened even further, her curls a wild mess beneath her crooked bonnet. "Indeed."

They were positively giddy and clearly not in their right minds.

"Oh, for goodness sake," Clara muttered. "We are not married yet." Leaving these two alone for but a few hours had led to catastrophic things *indeed*. She looked at Mabel. "What did you want to show me, darling?"

Blake's brows shot up. "Not married yet?"

"That's right." She nodded and focused on her daughter. "Please do show me what has you so excited, sweetheart."

"Come, it's this way!" Though Mabel tried to walk like a lady, she ended up dragging Clara along more often than not. "Just wait until you see!"

They passed whatever Blake and Maude were working on only to round the corner and come across something most unexpected.

"Saints above," she whispered, putting a hand to her heart. "Who did this?"

"Lord MacLauchlin." Mabel chuckled. "The one from Scotland, that is."

"It's…stunning." She smiled at the life-size rendition of Mabel shaped from a boxwood. The sculpture of her daughter held a flower and smiled further into the maze. Clara glanced at Blake when he and Maude joined them. "You did this, my lord? Truly?"

"Aye." His smile went from Maude and Mabel back to Clara. "With help, of course."

"You flatter us, my lord." Maude's gloved fingers fluttered up Blake's bicep before her mouth formed a small 'o' of surprise, and she pulled her hand away. "It was really mostly you."

"It truly was." Maude nodded graciously at Blake. "Our lord is talented with the trimmers, to be sure."

A noble talented with trimmers? How unexpected.

"To be sure," Clara echoed, unsure how to react to the most unusual situation. Should she tell her daughter this was unacceptable in decent society? Or cherish the smile on Mabel's face? The happiness in her eyes?

There really was no question.

Playing along, she pondered Mabel's sculpture. "And what, pray tell, put such a look of anticipation on her face? For she seems eager, does she not?"

"She truly is, Mother," Mabel assured. "For she is bringing a flower to the person she loves most."

"And who might that be?"

"Come." Mabel pulled her along, around the first corner of the maze, to the second, then third, walking a familiar path until she rounded the next bend and stopped short.

Clara gasped when she laid eyes on what her daughter had led her to.

"You, Mother." Mabel handed her a flower. "*You* are who I love most."

Chapter Eight

"Devil take you, cousin." Isaac scowled out the window at the maze below. "You planned this all along, didn't you?"

Naturally, Blake offered no response because he was down there. Or at least he had been several minutes ago. The point was he had, in his own discreet way, led Clara right to the last thing Isaac wanted her to see right now.

"Ah, so you are spying as usual," Blake declared upon entering unannounced. "I rather thought you might be, after being too cowardly to marry after all."

"Posting banns was in good form."

Blake snorted. "Posting banns was biding your time." He poured himself a whisky and lounged back on the sofa. His amused eyes were alight, and his hair a rumpled mess. "So, what happened between last night and today that made you put off the inevitable?"

"Nothing of consequence."

"Bollocks." Blake swigged his drink and kept eyeing Isaac with mirth. "Something happened, and now you are up here brooding and pining away for your long-lost love from the safe confines of your shadowed window."

"Why take Clara there?" he fumed, not entertaining his cousin's theories, however accurate they may be. "Why lead her to that sculpture so soon?"

"As opposed to giving her a few days to find it on her own?" Blake replied dryly. "And I did not lead her there. Lady Mabel did."

"You know bloody well what you did," Isaac growled.

"Actually, I do not." Blake swirled his whisky rather than down it as he usually would have by now. "Why don't you enlighten me?"

Isaac poured a whisky as well. "You do not need enlightening."

"Perhaps not," his cousin relented and shrugged. "Truth told, you should be thanking me, old chap. I merely picked up where you left off when you departed so hastily this morning."

"Hastily?" He frowned. "To what are you referring?"

"You know full well what." Blake took another sip, not afraid to tell him what he thought. "The moment you realized how happy you made wee Lady Mabel, you dashed off, terrified that she might want to join you and her mother. Worse yet, that if you lingered, she might end up liking you, which would inevitably let her down." He shook his head. "But then, as it turns out, taking her along would have disappointed her just as much."

On occasion, he loathed how well Blake knew him.

"You are wrong on all counts."

"I think not," Blake disputed. "I was there. I saw."

"You were nowhere to be found."

"Perhaps not me." He winked. "But most definitely, our old friend, Laurence."

Damn his butler. He talked too much.

Isaac braced his hand on the mantle and stared into the fire. While he'd been more comfortable with Mabel than expected, he did indeed fear being around her overly much. Of her liking him. Of him growing fond of her and, yes, somehow letting her down as he had his daughter. For that's how he'd felt when illness took Abigail, and there was nothing he could do to stop it. No amount of money in the world could save her.

"So, are you not the least bit curious how the duchess responded to your sculpture of her?" Blake asked, without a doubt switching the topic before Isaac dwelled on his daughter's death.

"No," he lied. "Besides, that sculpture, like other artwork here, is but a means of remembering those who touched this castle and our clan."

"Is that all it is?" Blake rolled his eyes. "I think a hedge sculpture of Clara's likeness in the very spot you—"

"We *nothing.*" He downed his whisky and turned his ever-darkening mood on his cousin. "You went too far today. And you did it without any right."

"No right, you say?" Blake narrowed his eyes. "When *I* am the one who saw that sculpture kept up season after season? *I* am the one by your side many a drunken night listening to you mourn the lass that got away?"

Isaac raked a hand through his hair and poured another whisky. "That was a long time ago."

"It *was.*" Blake finally downed his whisky as well. "Yet still, her ghost returned after you lost your wife, haunting your thoughts as though she had never left." He gestured at the window and, in turn, the sculpture beyond. "The proof sits right where you can see it whenever you want, Durham. Year after year, sitting there waiting, mourning just like you..."

"She is not mourning," Isaac defended softly, returning to the window. He sought out, as he too often did, the striking likeness of Clara that Blake had kept trimmed to perfection. "Just..."

When he trailed off, Blake filled in the rest.

"Just waiting and hoping." His cousin joined him, clasped his shoulder, and looked out as well. "She is not waiting anymore, old friend." He shook his head. "She is here, in this castle, and you would do well to remember that."

Blake lingered a few moments longer then left without another word, but that was for the best. Isaac's mood had grown too turbulent. Yes, he had asked his cousin to recreate the sculpture after his wife died, but that didn't make him showing it to Clara any easier.

She would have seen it eventually, sooner rather than later, considering her love of that maze, but he had thought perhaps…what? That *he* would show her? Lead her there beneath the moonlight? Remind her of their time together?

He had never forgotten sitting on the bench beside the bush that was now her likeness. How lovely she had appeared. Looking back on it now, he realized how very young they were. How foolish he was thinking to marry Clara when her father had yet to give Isaac his permission despite being asked.

Hesitation, as it turned out because he was determined to see Clara with Surrey.

Perhaps it was that very hesitation that made Isaac want to go around her father. To marry her even if it was in secret. He'd already tried proposing once at the pianoforte but lost his nerve, so he thought to try it again in the maze.

They had leaned close, so close, their breath mingling, only for a drunken fool to stumble by and ruin the moment. To this blasted day, he had yet to taste her sweet lips. To finally pull her into his arms and kiss her the way he had dreamt.

What had come from that moment and stayed with him many a lonely night after was the look on her face before they were interrupted. A look of longing and love he would never forget. One that had, despite her eventual treatment of him, sustained him over the years, making its way onto the face of the sculpture below.

"I'm sorry," he whispered into the silent room as though he spoke to her. "I am sorry for so much."

63

Namely that he had not stood up to her father. Perhaps if he had pressed him harder and not taken hesitation for an answer, things might have gone differently. Yet, deflated by his last visit to her house, he did not, and then it was too late.

But maybe in retrospect, considering his bad luck since, it had been for the best. Just like maintaining his distance now. Who knows, perhaps his hopelessness and lack of interest would make Clara realize that marrying him was not a good idea. He had told her he would protect her, and he would.

Marriage need not be the only way.

To that end, it was time to make himself scarce, which would normally mean being anywhere but here. Unfortunately, however, he had to remain close in case Kent eventually showed up.

Nevertheless, a man could vanish inside his own castle.

So he made it clear to his butler he had work to see over the next few weeks. He would dine in his study, and that would be that. He was not to be disturbed unless Blake popped in. Honestly, he had plenty to keep him busy, and it would give him time to think. If not to come up with a plan to get out of his upcoming marriage, then figure out which estate he would spend the majority of his time at over the next year.

What he didn't expect as the weeks wore on was the effect Clara's piano playing would have on him as it drifted through the castle up to his study. He noticed she only played when Mabel, Maude, and Blake were outside. In some strange way, despite servants being about, it felt like she played her sweet, haunting music solely for him. Almost as if she tried to coax him out of the dark place he had been in for so long.

Sometimes it saddened him, other times made him hopeful. As though he were saying goodbye and hello all at once. He ended up spending more time than he'd ever allowed himself thinking about Abigail, his brother, and even his late wife. When he wasn't recalling times spent with them, he wondered about those newly arrived, how they fared settling in. Despite Isaac pretending not to care, Blake stopped in occasionally, filling him in on just that.

"Lady Mabel keeps asking after you," Blake informed. "She remains eager to show you her hedge sculpture."

"She met me but once," he muttered.

"True." Blake snorted. "Therefore, I cannot imagine why she's so eager." He tapped the side of his glass and eyed Isaac with amusement, as he so often did lately. "It most certainly could not be because of the numerous new toys that keep arriving for her."

"I told Clara I would see to such." He continued signing paperwork, trying not to care.

Had she liked them that much?

"Well, you certainly have seen to such." Blake chuckled. "In abundance at that." There was no missing the mirth in his cousin's voice. "Why not just ask me?"

"Ask you what?"

"About Mabel's reaction to them."

He set aside a paper and started on another. "Because it's neither here nor there."

"So you say."

"You think me a liar?"

"Yes."

Isaac kept signing and changed the subject. "I have decided to attend the festival today, after all."

"I knew you would."

"You mean, you hoped."

"I mean, I knew."

Let him think what he would, however right he may be. "I assume you will be attending it with us?"

Blake's brow swept up. "And risk not seeing you navigate those you have so studiously avoided?" He offered a crooked grin. "I would not miss it for the world."

It turned out he meant that, too. More specifically, he meant to once again manipulate things.

So said what Isaac encountered when he joined everyone later.

Chapter Nine

"I do so like the way you think, my lord," Maude murmured to Blake just loud enough for Clara to hear. "Well played."

Rather than arrange for a single coach to carry everyone, Blake had ensured two horse-drawn phaeton carriages awaited them.

"Lord Durham will be joining us, right?" Mabel peered at the castle with longing. "I *do* hope so."

"I'm sure he will, darling." Despite Blake assuring Clara that Isaac would be attending, there was no way to be certain considering how he'd avoided them for over two weeks.

Day after day, she had awaited his presence so that they might talk, but he'd remained holed away. She nearly knocked on his door countless times but refrained, not entirely sure what to say.

Did he still care for her?

Had he all this time?

How else could it be, considering the sculpture of her?

Clara clearly remembered the evening it represented. She had dreamt of it often over the years. Not just the kiss they almost shared but the look in Isaac's eyes. She was sure he was going to ask her something. Ever since then, she had fantasized about what that might have been. Was he going to ask her to marry him? For he'd had that same light in his eyes days before at the pianoforte. As if he intended to say something important.

Yet the moment was interrupted, and he never continued.

Within the week, her father made arrangements for her to marry her late husband, and she heard little from Isaac after that. They no longer visited his estate, and he never came calling again.

Just like that, their friendship and anything else that might have been ended.

"There's Lord Durham!" Mabel perched her little pink parasol over her head and smiled widely. "I *knew* he would come."

Clara managed a warm smile upon Isaac's arrival. "Good day, my lord."

He looked handsome as ever in a dark waistcoat and matching top hat.

"Good day." Not quite meeting her eyes, he bowed to them. "You both look lovely."

"Why, thank you." Mabel curtsied, doing her best to exercise good manners rather than bubble over with excitement. "I very much look forward to this afternoon, my lord." She nodded graciously. "I am also very thankful for the gifts you have provided me."

"My pleasure, Lady Mabel."

Isaac assisted them into the carriage, and Mabel sat between them.

"I trust you have settled in well since last we spoke?" Isaac looked from Mabel to Clara. "That you want for nothing?"

"All is well," Clara lied. She *wanted* time alone with him. Now that he was finally out of his study, she intended to take advantage of it at the first opportunity. Until then, it seemed Blake and Maude were determined to put the three of them together.

She could admit she was glad, too, as they made their way down a dirt drive winding through the vibrant forest. Twinkling afternoon sunlight cut through the swaying trees, and multi-colored leaves rained down, lending a magical feel to the ride. Fortunately, Isaac appeared in one of his better moods and carried on quite the conversation with Mabel about the surrounding countryside and what it was like growing up here.

"You will not send me away, then?" her daughter said, forgetting good manners.

Clara tensed, wondering how this would go. She had meant to speak to him sooner about it but never got the chance. One could only hope he understood where she stood based on the stipulations she'd had with her late husband. If that were not enough, he above all should understand her reasoning because they had spoken about it years ago. How she had lost her own mother far too young and hoped her future daughter would not suffer the same someday.

"It almost sounds like you mean to keep her on at your estate," *he had said.*

"I do," she had confirmed. "I will."

And thus far, she had.

"Of course, you can stay on," Isaac replied to Mabel. "Where else would you be?"

The tension in Clara's shoulders eased as they continued chatting away. He was surprisingly good with Mabel, but then at one time, he had been lighthearted and entertaining with the young ones.

"Just *look*," Mabel exclaimed when they left the woodland behind, and a sprawling field of tents and revelry unfolded. "How *splendid*!"

That was an understatement.

Towns up this way were not overly large, so it seemed extravagant but clearly much welcomed by the locals. Every which way one looked there were things to see, from puppet shows to vendors selling wares to ventriloquists. Merry music played from various tents, and clowns meandered about, bringing smiles to children's faces.

"Isn't this wonderful?" Maude gushed the moment they joined them. Her eyes were every bit as round and wondrous as Mabel's. "Simply *marvelous.*"

"Indeed!" Blake held out the crook of his elbow to her daughter. "I believe I see a table of sweets ahead. Are you a fan of marzipan, Lady Mabel?"

"Oh, *yes*, my lord." She smiled widely and accepted his arm. "Very much so!"

With that, they were off with Isaac in trail, leaving her and Maude to follow. They linked arms, enjoying the late day sun warming their faces and the sugary treats and array of perfumes scenting the crisp air.

"My word is this not *something.*" Maude beamed at the odds and ends being sold. "And I dare say most unexpected up this way." A bit of deviousness curled her lips. "But then rumor has it the whole thing is well funded by an anonymous party."

Clara adjusted her bonnet's bow under her chin and eyed Maude. "Why do I get the feeling you know just who that is?"

"I may or may not," Maude teased before three, two, one, her secret was no more. "Or…" She whipped out her fan, leaned close, and spoke in a hushed but impressed voice. "I know precisely who it is, and we have the pleasure of his company." She went from pleased to critical in a flash. "So I suppose we can only be grateful he finally decided to join us."

She didn't blame Maude for being less than gracious, considering Isaac's absence these past few weeks. Even so, he *had* made it clear he would be keeping Clara at a distance, which evidently meant everyone else, too.

Clara perked her brows. "You mean to imply Lord Durham funded all this?"

"Not that you heard it from me, but yes, much of it." Maude leaned in a tad closer. "According to he who shall remain nameless,

Lord Durham started donating to this event when his daughter was old enough to come home and enjoy it." She gave Clara a pointed look. "If that is not heartwarming enough, it seems he donated more than usual this year. In fact, my anonymous source claims an extra donation was sent the very day he invited Mabel to attend the festival."

"Is that so?" she murmured, not sure what to make of that. "Do you think he did it for her?"

"I would hazard to say for you both." Maude gave Clara a dewy-eyed look from behind her fan. "For all his ghastly manners on occasion, it seems our lord might just have a romantic heart after all. How else can it be when he keeps his lady love alive with the skillful hands of a debonair Scot?"

She was referring to the sculpture in the maze.

Her eyes widened, and she giggled. "My goodness, that sounded all wrong, did it not?"

Clara couldn't help but chuckle in return before she grew serious, focusing on what else Maude had said. "So his daughter, Abigail, lived away from home?"

"So says my unknown source."

"Your source is Lord MacLauchlin."

"He may or may not be."

"He is."

"Whether he is or not, and could very well not be, my source claims Abigail was home rarely, per her mother's wishes," Maude revealed. "Sadly, it seems Lord Durham was of a different mind."

"He wanted her home?" Not so surprising based on what she had seen on the ride here. "How very unconventional."

"But seems to run in the family." Maude's gaze swept her way. "For despite our lord's closeted ways, you *are* a family now, are you not?"

71

"Not yet," she reminded. "Not by law. And then after that, perhaps only a year before we live separately."

"Plenty of time for things to get to where they need to be." Maude nodded once, sure of herself. "I expect it will take but a fraction of that time. Especially now that our lord is out and about, doing something so wholesome rather than closeted away, or worse yet, frequenting gambling dens to drown his grief."

"That seems quite specific." She shook her head. "And likely something Lord MacLauchlin should not have shared."

"Quite right," Maude replied. "If it was him."

"It was."

"Suffice it to say," Maude went on, "better that Lord Durham not brood at home, fearful of fanciful things, but enjoy some fresh air and good company."

Fearful of fanciful things? What did that mean?

Before Clara could ask, they rejoined the others, where Mabel enjoyed her marzipan and laughed at a puppet show.

Isaac handed Clara a piece of the tasty, almond-flavored confection. "I remember how much you enjoyed it."

"Thank you, my lord." She offered a small smile, recalling the first time he had bought her the treat. How she'd managed to get more on her dress and face than in her mouth. He fared no better, which led to a great deal of laughter. Ah, but the things one found amusing when young.

They fell in behind the others when they meandered along.

Though she got the sense Isaac wanted to speak with her, he remained silent. Did he know she had seen the sculpture? Highly likely. She suspected he knew every little thing that went on at his estate.

"You have done well with Mabel," he finally said, polishing off his sweet in record time. "She's lovely."

"Thank you." She smiled at her daughter, who tugged on Maude's sleeve about something. "She's been…" While she meant to say 'an angel' she said something else altogether. Truth had a way of coming out around him. "My saving grace."

"I can see that." He looked at Mabel fondly. "She has a way about her."

"She does."

"As do you," she swore he replied, but it was said too softly, and the noise of the behemoth tent they entered too loud.

"Heavens," she whispered, meeting Mabel's smile when she looked over her shoulder at Clara, then back at the spectacular sights. From the fire-eating man in his flaming red outfit to the acrobat rope dancers overhead, it was quite the display. One that easily rivaled the flamboyant shows at the Greenwich May, Southwark, and Bartholomew fairs.

She could only imagine how much Isaac had actually contributed. Undoubtedly a substantial amount. When Mabel declared she would like to sit and stay on a bit, Maude and Blake agreed, taken with the show.

"Why don't you two press on?" Blake grinned at them, without doubt Maude's co-conspirator in seeing Isaac and Clara spend time alone. "We will stay with Lady Mabel and join up with you in a bit."

"Are you sure?" Isaac asked, surprising her when he agreed to it.

"Oh, yes," Mabel responded. By the way she smiled at them, it seemed they were three peas in a pod. "We will be just fine."

As it happened, they did but not quite in the way she had hoped.

Chapter Ten

Though Isaac knew better, he found himself eager to spend time alone with Clara when it was the last thing he should do. Yet here he was, ushering her out of the tent at the first opportunity he got.

As always, she looked beautiful. Her lively curls peeked out from beneath a forest green silk bonnet that complimented her fur-trimmed pelisse, and the chilly air leant a rosy hue to her cheeks.

"My goodness, do you remember?" She bit her lower lip when they passed a fortune teller's tent. "We used to enjoy such amusements."

He couldn't help a small smile. "As I recall, you took them quite seriously."

"I suppose I did."

Neither mentioned what her last fortune had revealed. Perhaps she didn't even remember.

Ironically enough, she was told she would someday marry her one true love. While for the longest time he thought that just proved this sort of thing rubbish considering who she married, now, despite himself, he wondered. He'd yet to figure a way out of their upcoming nuptials, nor did she seem inclined to call it off due to his behavior, so unless she had a change of heart soon, they would be marrying.

That said, could he be her true love?

He should not think it, let alone wish it.

Unable to help himself, he repeated the very words he'd said the first time they came across a fortune teller. "Do you want to go in?"

"Do you?" she replied, just as she had back then.

He grinned. "I asked first."

She smiled, playing along. "I suppose I do."

"Very good."

As she had when they exited the acrobat tent, she seemed a bit breathless at his proximity when he touched her lower back and escorted her into the fortune teller's tent. Or perhaps it was just wishful thinking. His own fanciful desires. Erotic yearnings that had plagued him since the moment she stepped foot on his estate.

Though he had enjoyed a dalliance or two since he'd lost his wife, none were Clara, so he had moved on, eventually coming to the conclusion he might never feel that kind of passion again. Despite never laying with or even kissing her, there had always been this heat between them. This intense attraction he knew she felt, too.

The air inside the tent smelled of aromatic, exotic oils and sweetly scented smoke. Candlelight flickered over dark purple damask wall coverings, creating ominous shadowed corners designed to appear mysterious. Brightly colored pillows were strewn about on low, plush, Romanian-style furnishings.

"Ah, yes, here you are," a too-thin woman with ruby lips and large, charcoal-lined eyes murmured. She bowed her head and gestured that they sit at a small pedestal table in front of her. "Please sit. I have been waiting for you, my lord and lady."

Their clothing gave away their nobility. She also likely knew who Isaac was, considering he was the festival's primary benefactor. So he imagined she would put on quite the show.

Nonetheless, they were here to be amused, so they did as asked.

"Ladies first." The diviner looked at Clara. "Give me your hands, my dear."

Clara did, and the woman closed her eyes, breathing deeply before she studied the fine lines on Clara's palms. She traced one with her long crimson fingernail. "Such sadness so young." Then she traced another. "But love, too. A chance at escape." The woman closed her eyes again before narrowing one eye on another line. "Followed by more sadness." She flinched. "A harsh prison." A whimsical smile curled her lips. "Then a new special kind of love." Her gaze rose to Clara's face. "That of a mother."

While Isaac appreciated a good show, he grew warier as the reading continued. This fortune teller knew far too much. Who had told her all this?

"You need not keep wondering, madam." The woman's gaze grew tender. "You already know the answer to what weighs most on your mind." She gave Clara a knowing look. "All you truly fear now are the words unknown. Those that may never come."

What weighed on Clara's mind most? And what bloody words unknown?

The diviner wiggled her fingers that he give her his hands. "Now, you, my lord."

Though suspicious, the curious light in Clara's lovely eyes kept him playing along, and he rested his hands on the table. Benefactor money aside, he was well known in these parts, so everything the fortune teller said was likely common knowledge.

Point in fact, how she led out.

"My condolences, my lord," the woman whispered, tracing the lines on his left hand first. "I see your loss has been unending." She closed her eyes and breathed deeply. "Yet now the fork in the road becomes a singular path again." Her gaze opened and locked on his face. "The path that was always meant to be yours."

She clearly knew Clara had resided near his estate for a time. That they had become acquainted. Then likely even heard rumors that they had loved one another in their youth.

76

The woman allowed him to pull one hand away but held the other firmly. Her gaze remained on his face for a moment before it dropped to his palm. "Only you can determine how much she is worth when danger comes." Her eyes rose. "Remember, *that* is what it is for."

"What do you mean?"

"You will know."

He frowned, uneasy for no good reason. "I would rather you just tell me."

"Yet I cannot."

"But of course." Because she didn't know. This was but a ruse— utter nonsense.

And he was feeding right into it like a fool.

"I think we have heard enough." He put a coin in her jar and led Clara out, saying over his shoulder crisply, "I bid you good day, madam."

"I don't think she meant any harm, my lord," Clara said softly as they made their way through the merry people. The sun had just set, and torches sizzled to life.

"All is well," he replied instinctively, sensing Clara's sudden distress. "I was but mildly offended by her opportunistic ways."

"Everyone must get by somehow," she reminded, clearly trying to calm him, though he was barely rattled. "It was merely for our amusement, anyway."

"And were you amused?" He gentled his voice, feeling that same sense of frustration he'd felt the first night she arrived. To hell and back with Surrey for doing this to her. For somehow subduing her.

Because he most certainly had.

"I *was* amused." Her gaze flickered to his face when he steered her closer to him in the thickening crowd. "At least when we first arrived."

He appreciated her honesty. That she felt confident—safe—enough to express it. She had enjoyed the fortune teller but not so much his reaction to her. Truth be told, he wasn't entirely sure why he'd grown miffed to begin with, considering it was all just a show. Maybe it was as simple as not liking the thought of a stranger knowing so much about him. Or perhaps the idea of potential danger anywhere near Clara when she had initially sought him out because of Kent.

Either way, he understood why Clara's amusement had faded.

"Point taken." He continued navigating them through the crowd until they reached the end of the tents. A bonfire crackled on the meadow, stars twinkled overhead, and people danced. "So we will leave all that behind us."

"Probably for the best." Yet, she seemed tentative. "If that is your wish."

"Is it not yours?" He considered her. "And please don't just tell me what you think I want to hear."

Because he realized in the carriage the day they put up their banns, she could easily revert to doing just that.

"Well," she confessed, "outside of the perplexing outcome of my reading, I found our fortune teller rather spot on."

"So something weighs on your mind above all else?" He arched his brows. "Something you already know the answer to?"

"Perhaps," she murmured, her gaze anywhere but on him. "I just thought her…"

"Thought her what?" he prompted when she hesitated.

"I cannot say really," she replied vaguely, her cheeks pinkening. "Just worth listening to, I suppose."

He sighed, frustrated she would not be franker with him but on the same token, recognizing that he remained equally vague. Not just that, but prompting her to share more could very well pull them closer—the opposite of what should happen.

Or so he kept trying to convince himself.

Truly, though, despite how much he could admit to still caring for her, it changed nothing when it came to his bad luck. To his fear that something might happen to her and Mabel if he let them get too close.

Despite all that, words just rolled off his tongue.

Questions he longed to have answered.

"Why did you not come down to speak with me all those years ago?" He cursed himself for asking but truly wanted to know. *Had* to know.

She frowned. "To what are you referring?"

When he hesitated, wondering how blunt he should be, she went on. "Come down when, my lord?"

Just have out with it. Tell her what you have long been curious about.

"I came calling," he finally revealed, saying more than he probably should. "After the last time we saw one another, and I learned of your upcoming marriage to the Duke of Surrey, I came to ask you to reconsider."

"You did?" Her brows pinched. "I never received word of it. Did you announce your visit first? Was I even home?"

"Your butler sent a maid up to tell you of my arrival," he replied. "Not only was it relayed to me you didn't wish to receive me, but I heard you say such from upstairs."

"No." Clara shook her head. "Never." She frowned and thought about it, eyeing him curiously. "Is there any reason my father would have wanted to keep you away? For those were his butler and maids in his service."

He clenched his jaw and remained vague. "I'm sure your father knew of my intentions."

She tilted her head. A flash of challenge lit her eyes. "And what were those?"

"That I might keep courting you, of course," he lied.

He should just tell Clara he'd asked her father for her hand, but what difference would it make now? The more curious, better yet heartbreaking thing, had always been her turning him away in the end.

"I mean no offense," she looked at him dubiously, "but you, a marquess, hoped to merely keep *courting* me when a duke had asked for my hand in marriage?" She pressed her lips together as if holding back so much more than she said. "Surely you knew my father well enough to know despite your rank being just beneath my late husband's, it would not be enough."

"Evidently." Isaac tried to keep contempt from his voice. "Despite my family's vast wealth and long ties with your own family." He cocked a brow, getting back to the point. "Yet last I knew, a father cannot order his daughter to marry someone against her will."

"Then you do not remember my father very well, my lord." Anger and hurt flashed in her eyes. Rather than let her emotions get the better of her, though, Clara focused on the initial conversation. "If you came calling after my marriage was arranged, I imagine the servants were told to keep you at bay no matter what it took. Mimicking my voice would not have been that difficult. Not all my ladies were French. One or two were English."

"Bloody bugger," he cursed, then apologized for the slander, divulging more than intended. "Was I so easily duped by your overbearing father?" He scowled, again saying more than he probably should. "Though it is safe to say I was not at my best."

That was putting it mildly.

Clara was about to reply when the others rejoined them with cups in hand.

"We brought you some mulled wine," Blake announced. He and Maude handed them each one. Mabel had cider.

Clara thanked them, then smiled at her daughter. "Did you have fun?"

"Yes." Mabel's round eyes shimmered with excitement. "Such fun!" She looked at everyone dancing. "Might we dance, Mother?"

"Yes, darling." She gestured at Mabel's cup. "You must finish that first, though."

Everyone but Isaac ended up joining in the merriment, but that was just as well. He needed time to come to terms with Clara's revelation.

She had not turned him away.

That had not been her voice.

While it seemed hard to believe now, the cold hard truth was a young man that deeply in love had trouble seeing reason when he felt rejected. Trouble seeing beyond his own turbulent emotions to good sense.

So he supposed only one question remained.

Did Clara ever tell her father what *she* really wanted? Better yet, would she have married Isaac had he asked her? Something he decided, despite his need to keep away from her, he would get the answer   to   that   very   night.

Chapter Eleven

By the time everyone made it home later that evening, Clara was happier than she had been in ages. Though Isaac hadn't joined in the dancing, he seemed in better spirits overall.

"Do not wake her," Isaac said when they arrived at his estate. Mabel had dozed off almost the moment they got in the carriage, her head resting against his shoulder. "I will carry her up to bed."

The gesture both touched and surprised her. But then it seemed he was full of surprises tonight. She was relieved, and even a bit saddened to hear he had not been willing to let her go so easily all those years ago. That he'd cared enough, however pointless his venture likely would have been. How might that conversation have gone when he came calling? What would he have said? Would he have asked for her hand right then and there? For she swore, he had meant to twice before that.

She had so many questions—things she needed to understand.

"You will be joining us for supper, I hope?" Blake asked Clara. He had Maude on one arm but offered her his other. "Lord Durham's cook always provides a tasty fare at this hour."

"But of course." She took his arm, and they headed up the stairs. "What a truly lovely night it has been thus far."

"I could not agree more." Maude noted Isaac vanishing inside with Mabel. "A lovely evening all the way around."

"Indeed." Blake eyed the same. "I would not be surprised to see Lord Durham more after tonight."

"I do hope so." Maude cocked her head. "What of this eve? Do you think he will rejoin us?"

"I think it's highly likely."

Clara could only pray. She wanted to talk. Sift through things. See if there was hope for them. They had misunderstood how things ended years ago. Or better put, didn't realize how much the other still cared.

Which begged the question, were those feelings still there?

Perhaps she should just tell him how accurate the fortune teller had been. What harm could it do? A great deal, she realized, considering she would be laying her heart bare.

It turned out Blake was right, and Isaac did return downstairs, reporting all was well with Mabel. Music floated in from the adjoining room as they enjoyed a light fare of cold meats and cheeses served with bread and rolls. Sweets and chilled champagne followed.

"That was, as always, delightful, Durham," Blake declared when they finished. His gaze swept over the lot of them. "The night is still young. Might we get in some whist and dancing?"

Maude smiled. "I would like nothing more, Lord MacLauchlin."

Despite her status, Maude had become a permanent fixture at meals, spending a noticeable amount of time with Blake when not caring for Mabel.

Clara was surprised when Isaac continued on with the three of them. More shocked still when they made their way into the piano room. Though not nearly as large as the ballroom, it had an area for dancing and a rather nice card table.

She couldn't help but wonder if they were there on purpose. Though a hired musician played the pianoforte, it almost felt like

Isaac tempted her by bringing them here. Had he heard her play over the past few weeks? Had it affected him like she'd hoped it might?

For if music could heal her, it could heal him, too.

First on the agenda, though, was not her potentially playing the piano, but some good fun. The moment Blake and Maude teamed up to play against them, Clara knew she and Isaac had them. Or so she hoped if they still played half as good as they once did together.

After each player was dealt thirteen cards, the game advanced clockwise, and they played the next thirteen tricks while chatting. Though Isaac's demeanor was more reserved, and he wasn't as talkative as he once was with her, he seemed somewhat improved. Or at least more present than he had been thus far.

While tempted, she had refrained from taking Maude aside to ask what *fanciful things* he was fearful of when off brooding the past few weeks. Based on how her friend had said it earlier, she suspected it directly related to Clara and perhaps even Mabel.

"I see you two have played this together before," Blake eventually muttered when points were counted, and Clara and Isaac won.

"A time or two." Isaac grinned and arched a brow at Blake. "Perhaps a rubber of whist?"

"Why would I go best out of three games with the likes of you two and lose again?" Blake stood, bowed to Maude, and held out his hand. "When I might just as easily dance with a lovely woman."

Maude smiled demurely and slipped her hand into his.

Blake signaled the pianist. "A waltz, good sir."

The man nodded and played the latest German waltz.

Isaac's gaze found Clara. "Another game, perhaps?"

"No, I should probably retire."

"Or," he stood when she stood, "you could stay for a dance?"

Caught off guard, she eyed his outstretched hand. It had been a long time since they danced together. Since she experienced how he could make her feel when he pulled her close.

"Just one dance, madam." His gaze softened on her. "If I remember correctly, we danced as well as we play cards."

"We did." How could she say no? She slipped her hand into his. "It would be my pleasure, my lord."

When he wrapped his arm around her waist and stepped closer, her breath caught at the strength and heat of his body. He smelled faintly of the starch used to press his shirt and a rich, clean, citrusy cologne. Not overwhelming by any means, Isaac had never been a dandy, but subliminal and masculine.

Their gazes met, and she swore his breath hitched as well.

She might wonder where his heart lay, but there could be no questioning the desire he still felt for her. It was right there in his steady gaze. In the flare of his pupils and tightening of his body. As though he held back from yanking her even closer. From touching her in all the delicious ways she had once fantasized he would. Kissing her with intense, untamed passion.

The moment he swirled her onto the dance floor, the years fell away, and they moved perfectly together. Just as it had back then, the room faded, and only he existed. His gaze remained on her face as they twirled, their steps as one. Around and around, never missing a beat. Her pulse fluttered at the delicate intensity of their movements. At how it seemed neither could look away.

Her heart slammed into her throat.

Blazing heat curled through her.

A throbbing ache pooled below.

One she had not felt in far too long. A need that made her weak in the knees.

She wasn't sure when the song finished, only that she wished it had gone on forever. Kept them locked in what blossomed between them. Feelings that were both old and new, all at once. Made of the fondness they once shared and a deeper connection. A bond formed not just from the trials they had faced apart, but a future they might share together, if he pushed past his demons and whatever held him back.

"Will you play the pianoforte?" he murmured when the last note drifted off. He kept her close. "Here and now. For me?"

"Yes," she managed, breathless. If it helped bring them closer, she would time and time again. She glanced at Blake and Maude. "Do you mind?"

"Not at all." Maude clasped her hands together in delight and smiled widely. "That would be absolutely divine." Excitement lit her eyes when she looked at Blake. "Oh, I simply cannot wait. Can you?" Before he had a chance to respond, she looked at Clara and went on. "I have longed to hear you play, for you speak so fondly of it."

They hadn't heard Clara play their first night here because they had already retired. Since then, she'd only played when they were gone, wanting those times for her and Isaac. A means not only to aid him in navigating whatever haunted him but perhaps to help the two of them find their way back to each other.

Blake smiled at Clara and made a hand flourish toward the pianoforte. "Then, by all means, Your Grace."

She thanked the pianist when he held out the seat for her and cherished the feel of sitting at the pianoforte once more. Eager to feel the keys beneath her fingers, desperate to hear their sweet sound, she closed her eyes and considered what she wanted to play.

Something that matched how she felt right now.

Not somber but hopeful. Happy but careful. Elated yet fearful. Would her lord remain close? Or would he flee back into the dark recesses of his castle once more? Would she open her eyes and not see him again for days? Or would he be right here, watching her, desperate for the rest of their lives to begin?

Clara had no idea she was playing until she opened her eyes and saw him right there. Right next to her with the same awed expression he had worn when they first met. Watching her as though he'd never seen anything so precious. Heard anything so magnificent.

Though unable to play, she had written this particular song years ago when remembering their time together. The passion she had felt for him made its way into the notes. A sense of breaking free as their friendship grew and became something more. Of flying beyond the cage one found themselves in. Then the bars that slammed down between them the moment her father married her off to another. The heartbreak of knowing it was over.

Her fingers flew over the keys, sometimes coming down harder, other times much softer. She couldn't look away from Isaac if she tried. All her feelings poured out through her music. Everything she felt, then and now and the years in between. The sadness of losing her mother, then the happiness of finding him. The joy he had brought into her life. Then the shadows that fell when fate took her elsewhere—yet renewed joy in meeting her daughter.

By the time the last note echoed through the room, one could hear a pin drop. Isaac's gaze never left her face. Not once. Rather, he seemed enchanted and lost, immersed in what she had given him.

"By God, that was something," Blake finally managed, interrupting their reverie. "Was it not?"

Only when she heard a host of 'yes, my lords' did she realize how many she had drawn. Servants who nodded and smiled at her before going about their business.

"Thank you, madam," Isaac said softly, seeming to gather himself. "That was…breathtaking."

"To say the least," Maude agreed. "What was that you played? It was so very moving."

"I have yet to name it." She smiled and nodded thanks to them all. "I'm glad you enjoyed it."

When she stood, of the mind to retire, Isaac held out his elbow, surprising her yet again. "Perhaps a midnight stroll before you go?"

Eager to finally talk, she slipped her arm into his. "I would like that."

They bid Blake and Maude goodnight and ended up not roaming the hallways but going outside.

"What a beautiful evening." She admired the swollen moon peeking out from behind fast-moving clouds. "From start to finish."

The wind was starting to pick up, and thunder rumbled in the distance, but it made no difference. Just being here with him made everything perfect.

"Without a doubt, the eve was unforgettable." He steered her through the gardens. "I thought perhaps we could enjoy your maze once more."

She perked her brows and smiled. "My maze?"

"I always thought so," he murmured. "You seemed to love it more than most."

"I suppose I did." What of his wife? Daughter? Did they not enjoy it? "But then, I fell in love with it when young. But a child."

"I know." A gentle smile hovered on his lips. "I was there."

"Yes, you were."

"And I am here now." He led her through the maze in a familiar direction. "Or at least I'm trying to be."

"I see that."

"Do you?"

"I believe so, my lord."

"Isaac," he corrected. "My name is Isaac."

"I know," she murmured, caught by emotion when they rounded the corner and stopped near her sculpture. "But it's not proper to call you such."

"It is when we are alone." His gaze found the sculpture. "I should explain…"

"I wish you would." She swallowed hard and looked at him. "Why is this here? For it seems quite…"

When she trailed off, he continued. "Telling?"

"Very."

"Because it is."

Telling of what precisely, though? What he felt then or now?

"Was it here when your wife was here?"

"Yes, but overgrown." He urged her to sit beside him on the bench. "I'm not that callous."

"I would hate to think it."

"Then do not." He looked from the sculpture back to her. "What do you see when you look at it, Clara?"

Her pulse leapt at the sound of her name on his lips.

"Hope," she whispered, thinking of the last night they spent here.

"Hope of what?"

"I think you know." Her gaze drifted to the sculpture. To the eager look on her young face that he might finally ask her to marry him. "I think you saw it when you had your cousin portray it so well."

"I thought I did, but I have second-guessed myself often since."

"I'm sorry to hear that."

"Would you have said yes?" He tilted her chin until their gazes aligned, startling her with the warmth of his hand. His tender touch. The pained look in his eyes.

"If you had asked for my hand in my marriage?"

"Yes." He cupped her cheek. "Would you have?"

"How can you for a moment wonder?" She swallowed hard. "How can you—"

That's all she got out before he took the words right out of her mouth and finally did something she had waited ages for him to do.

89

Chapter Twelve

Isaac meant not to do it, but the moment he touched Clara's soft cheek, he had to kiss her. When she implied that she would have said yes to his proposal years ago, he wasted no more time.

While he'd imagined the feel of her lips beneath his too many times to count, it paled in comparison to the real thing. To how she melted against him and twisted her fist in his shirt. How her mouth opened beneath his, exploring and tentative, then eager and desperate. Though he kept his kisses soft at first, gentle and curious, they soon became more passionate, and their tongues tangled.

When she offered a throaty little groan, he pulled her onto his lap, dug his hand into her tempting curls, and kissed her harder still. She tasted of sweet wine and erotic fantasies. Of all the things he wanted to do to her. To make her feel.

Things he could do right now.

It was dark. They were alone. He could slide his hand up beneath her skirts along her silky thigh. Touch her soft folds. Build her desire. Press his fingers into her tight, hot…

"Oh," she gasped, pulling back when several heavy raindrops hit them.

"Damnation," he muttered under his breath, mostly because he was so painfully aroused. Should he take her to the veranda, not all that far off? Yank up her skirts and finally sink into her sweet heat? Hear her groans of pleasure? Lose himself in her lovely little body?

Though tempted, he knew it was a bad idea. If he did, he might never stop. Never let her free of him and, in turn, his curse. Not when he wanted her with a ferociousness that would make it impossible to let go.

What had he been thinking bringing her out here? Implying that he wanted to get closer to her? No longer keep her at a distance? It seemed he'd been cast beneath a spell. Ensorcelled by her music. Not thinking straight.

He was now, though, thanks to the sudden deluge.

So back to the castle it would be.

Even though he held his jacket over her head as they raced inside, it did little good. They were soaked by the time they got through the front door. In any other reality, he would carry her upstairs, strip her down, and warm her up in the best way possible.

But alas, he would do no such thing.

If he did, that would be it. Her fate sealed. She seemed to see it on his face, too, because her humor from the run inside faded when she looked at him.

"A warm bath will be drawn for you straight away." He nodded to Mrs. Angus that she see it done. Bowing slightly at the waist, he kissed the back of Clara's hand, making it clear they would be going their separate ways. "I bid you goodnight, madam."

Disappointment flashed in her eyes. "Goodnight to you as well, my lord."

Clara followed the maid, only to pause at the bottom of the stairs and give him her profile. "Just so you know, the fortune teller was absolutely right. Only one question weighs on my mind, and I think...*hope* you understand what that might be now." She glanced back at him. "I hope you understand how I feel. What I hope you might feel, too."

She left it at that and went upstairs.

Frustrated, he stared after her, wishing he could push past his fears and give her what she wanted, what they both wanted. But how could he risk it? How could he subject her and Mabel to his rotten luck? He would never forgive himself if something happened to them. He may not have known her daughter very long, but he could safely say she touched his heart. That he could see being a father to her. Raising her as his own.

A subject he grumbled about the next morning when he and Blake were out hunting. "I should have given my estate over to Dove-Lyon and been done with it."

"Because you have grown fond of a little girl and remain in love with her mother?" Blake rolled his eyes. "Yes, best to give up everything straight away so that you need not suffer."

"I think *in love* might be a stretch," he muttered.

"More like an understatement."

"You must admit, I'm not very lucky." Isaac swung down from his horse, sat with his back against a tree, and set his gun aside, not in the mood for hunting after all. "Perhaps, as some whisper, I am cursed."

"You have lost people, my friend." Blake swung down from his mount as well. "Perhaps more than most, but sadly these things happen. Not because you are cursed but simply due to a run of unfortunate circumstances." He shook his head. "Such should not keep you from finding happiness again." He sat and handed Isaac a flask. "And the duchess and wee Mabel make you happy when you allow them to."

They did. Very much so.

"Perhaps your hesitation has less to do with believing in fanciful curses, but something else," Blake pondered. "Perhaps fear of risking your heart again."

"When did I ever risk my heart?" He scowled at the flask after he took a swig. "Water?"

"Yes." Blake waved it away. "Plenty of time for stronger stuff later."

"Since when do you care what time of day it is?"

"Since I started enjoying my evenings a tad more."

He perked his brows. "Miss Maude, then?"

"Miss Maude," Blake confirmed. He grinned, really rather enthusiastic, Isaac realized. "I find her entertaining."

He arched his brows even higher. "Just how entertaining?"

"Very."

Was Blake falling in love? Isaac had been rather closeted the past few weeks, but had he missed so much?

"She has no status," Isaac reminded. "Nor do I imagine she comes with a dowry."

"Neither of which I need."

"God's teeth," Isaac exclaimed. Now that he was focusing less on his own woes, he noted that Blake truly did seem changed. "You feel that strongly then?"

"I would not be considering it otherwise." Blake shrugged. "Naturally, I intend to court her first, but yes, I see Miss Maude being a good match for me." He tilted his head in acquiescence. "Granted, time will tell for certain, but I can say with confidence I have never met another quite like her."

Isaac imagined not. Maude was uniquely…Maude. Truth be told, Blake held his own title and wanted for nothing financially, so there was no reason not to do as he pleased.

"Then I wish you the very best." He clasped his cousin on the shoulder and grinned. "Have you made your intentions known yet?"

"No, I thought to speak with her this evening." Blake looked at him in question. "Perhaps you would join us for another night of revelry? Dinner and some cards? I would hate for Duchess Surrey to be alone when we excuse ourselves for a time."

"How long a time?" He narrowed his eyes, sensing a dash of manipulation. "What are you up to, cousin?"

"Whatever do you mean?" Blake stood and stretched. "Is it so wrong of me to ask you to keep your future wife company?"

"Some might say yes, considering I'm trying to keep her at a distance."

"And how did that go last night?" Blake offered a crooked grin and swung onto his horse. "For it seemed every time you had a chance to push her away, you only pulled her closer."

He mounted his horse as well. "And how would you know if you were so enamored with Miss Maude?"

"It would have been impossible not to notice." Blake sighed and considered him. "Even if it had not been, keeping up the duchess's sculpture is telling." His brows swept up. "More so, you had plenty of time to cut it down before she arrived, yet you chose not to. Rather, you left it knowing full well she would find it."

"So what if I did?" He steered his horse alongside Blake's. "It makes no difference to the outcome of things."

"Blast it, man, but it does!" Blake's mouth slanted down. "It makes all the difference, and it's long past time you realize that."

"Long past? She's only been here a few weeks."

"But in your heart for far longer," Blake countered. "On your mind every time we went to the Lyon's Den and spied on her late husband." His brows whipped together. "Have you told her yet? Have you told her how you stalked Surrey for so long? Because your actions speak to a man whose concern for her never waned. It speaks to great love indeed!" Before Isaac could reply, Blake spurred his horse, throwing over his shoulder, "Think about that, my lord. Moreover, think about how luck turned in your favor the moment she came back into your life."

He couldn't remember the last time Blake had grown so heated. But then he supposed it was to be expected. His cousin had been there for him through the thick of it after he lost his family. He had also kept Clara's memory alive with a set of trimmers and tirelessly listened to Isaac ramble about her when in his cups.

"You did well to set her from your mind when you married," Blake *had commented on one of those drunken nights. He'd narrowed one eye, then the other trying to focus on Isaac. "Or have you?"*

"Yes." He had nodded and then shook his head. "No." Scowling, he'd called for another round. "Of course, I didn't think of her. I was married."

He knew his cousin would not have blamed him if he did, considering Isaac's marriage had not been one of love but of convenience. Or so it had always seemed. He'd tried to make his wife happy, he really had, but she'd been distant from the onset. Love never blossomed. For that matter, it never came close. The only real affection he'd gotten out of the union was his daughter. Sadly, even that was rare because his wife had insisted she live away.

So truly, when it came to children remaining home, he and Clara were a perfect match.

A match in many things. From dancing to games to general conversation. They genuinely enjoyed one another's company. And there could be no doubt of their attraction to one another. The simmering passion. Hell, he'd been up all night fantasizing about what he would have done had he only brought her to bed. The idea of finally spreading her slender thighs and pressing deep into her moist, welcoming sheath had him so aroused he'd ended up giving up on sleep altogether.

While he should be grateful Clara was nowhere to be found when he returned to his castle, he found himself hoping he might run into her anyway. There was no sign of her, however, so he strolled around the back only to run into Mabel.

She curtsied and smiled up at him from beneath her pink bonnet. "Good morning, my lord."

He tipped his hat, charmed despite himself. "Good morning, Lady Mabel. I trust you slept well?"

"I did, thank you."

"Very good." He glanced around. "What are you doing roaming about?" Just as her mother would have at that age. "Where is Miss Maude?"

"Just that way, preparing a school lesson for me." She pointed in a random direction, smiling all the wider. "I thought whilst she was doing that, I would check on things out this way."

He couldn't help but grin, considering how close they were to the maze. "And what would those things be?"

"Mine and Mother's sculptures." She tilted her head. "Would you care to join me?"

Best not. Carry on. Do not dally. Nothing good can come of allowing himself to care.

"I would love to." He held out his elbow. "Shall we?"

"We shall, good sir." She slipped her arm into his. "It's a lovely day, is it not?"

"It is," he agreed.

Though gusty, the air was tepid.

"You must enjoy living here." Though excitement lit her eyes, Mabel remained calm and cordial as she had likely been taught. "It is a wondrous place."

"Indeed." They walked through the outer edges of the garden. "With an equally wondrous history."

"Do tell." Her gaze grew wide. "If you would not mind, that is. Just a *wee* bit as Uncle Blake would say."

Uncle Blake, was it? Well, why not?

"Just a wee bit then, aye, lassie?" Isaac replied, embracing a brogue for her benefit. He smiled and contemplated the many tales he had heard over the years. "Well, there is rumor that my ancestor was rescued from this very castle by her one true love." He picked a vibrant pink aster flower and handed it to her. "That they fell in love here and even once passed through this very garden before they escaped into the night."

"Oh, *my*." She thanked him for the flower and sniffed it. "Where did he take her? And were they ever caught?"

"He took her all the way to Scotland." Isaac shrugged. "As to them being caught, I could not say." He winked. "The fact that I'm here over four hundred years later speaks to a successful outcome, though."

"Four hundred years," Mabel whispered, thinking about that, quite a romantic at heart it seemed. "How lovely and to be expected, I suppose."

"Why is that?"

"Because rescuing one's true love runs in the family." She smiled and glanced in the direction of her mother's sculpture. "Or else we would not be here."

He wasn't entirely sure what to say to that. Had Clara said something? Had she told her daughter how close they had once been? Or did the sculpture make it clear enough even to a child? More importantly, and far more concerning, why did Mabel consider Isaac she and her mother's rescuer? Something, though tempted, he could not simply come out and ask. He could, however, inwardly fume at Surrey yet again, for he was undoubtedly at the heart of it. So said the rumors.

"I'm glad I could assist, Lady Mabel," he replied, figuring it best to keep things simple.

Yet it seemed Mabel was of another mind, her words surprising.

"Thank you, Lord Durham." She picked a flower and handed it to him. "And thank you for loving Mother, for she deserves it ever so much."

While tempted to say he did not love Clara, he chose not to lie so bluntly to the child. For he suspected, despite her young age, Mabel would see right through it. Yet little did he anticipate her cleverness when he replied with what made sense, thinking things would be left at that.

"My pleasure, Lady Mabel."

Her eyes lit up again. "So, you really do love Mother?"

"I…what I mean to say…" he stammered.

So caught up that he had no idea what to do when Mabel took immediate action and did the last thing he expected.

Chapter Thirteen

"How positively *lovely*." Maude clapped her hands together and eyed the stunning gowns that had been delivered to Clara's room. "Your future husband has exquisite taste, and I dare say, knows the right colors for you." She eyed Clara before fingering the delicate material of one of the dresses. "If he spoils you this much whilst off brooding most of the time, I cannot imagine what wonders he'll bestow when he finally admits he loves you and sweeps you off your feet."

Before Clara could get a word in edgewise, Maude tittered on. "How did he ever get these made so swiftly?" Her eyes widened once again. "Dear me, you do not think they are his late wife's?" She sniffed the material, her brows puckering in concentration before her features relaxed, and she nodded with unnecessary assurance at Clara. "Let me be the first to tell you, all is well. These are brand new." She scrunched her nose and fanned her hand as though doing away with a foul odor. "I have delicate senses, so would know otherwise."

"But of course you would." She bit back a small smile and fingered one of the silk dresses as well. Isaac had spared no expense, getting her measurements perfect.

"Though one has to wonder," Clara murmured, speaking aloud without realizing it.

Maude perked a brow. "Wonder what?"

"About this." She handed an elegantly written note to Maude that had been tucked in with the dresses. "Do you notice anything strange?"

Maude looked over the order list before her brows shot up. "Well, I'll be. The date is all wrong."

"It is," she agreed. "For that implies, these dresses were commissioned to be made one day after I visited Mrs. Dove-Lyon."

"It does." A silly little smile hovered on her friend's mouth. "Which can only mean one thing."

"That he knew my size," she said softly. "Despite not having seen me for years."

Maude's eyes rounded. "I *knew* it!"

"Knew what?"

"That Lord MacLauchlin was hedging at something the other night." She leaned closer and whispered as though someone else was in the room. "I do believe your Lord Durham has kept an eye on you for some time, madam."

A strange little thrill shot through her.

"Surely not." Could it be? She frowned at Maude. "And what precisely was Lord MacLauchlin hedging at?"

Maude's lips twisted, and she shrugged before becoming overly interested in the stitching on one of the dresses. "Whoever did this is *very* good at—"

"Maude." She cocked her head. "What did Lord MacLauchlin imply?"

"Sweet saints, you *are* persistent." Maude looked left and right, only to confirm that, yes, as had been the case for some time, they were very much alone. "Well, I'm not one to gossip, but I suppose given you are my very dearest friend, that Blake," her fingers fluttered to her mouth. "Dear me, how inappropriate. What I mean to say is my lord, or *laird*, as he claims is the proper way to say it." She pursed her lips. "You try now. *Laird*. You must roll your 'r' just so."

"Maude?"

"Yes?"

"What did lord, *laird*," she granted, rolling her 'r' just fine, "MacLauchlin imply?"

"Oh, yes, back to that."

She rolled her eyes. "Yes, *that*."

"Well," Maude huffed, "and, again, not to gossip, but it seems our lords visited Mrs. Dove-Lyon's establishment quite regularly."

"I gathered that," she replied dryly.

Maude slid her a look. "What else did you gather?"

"What else should I have gathered?"

"For starters, did you get the impression your lord took advantage of Mrs. Dove-Lyon's female clientele?" She whipped out her fan. "That he indulged in," the fan started fluttering, and her cheeks pinkened, "unmentionables."

"One would have thought by his behavior." She considered what Bessie had implied. "Though Mrs. Dove-Lyon did say something curious."

"Pray tell?"

"She led me to believe his ogling women was all for show."

"And I dare say it was." Maude's fan picked up its pace. "In fact, I would say your future husband frequented the Lyon's Den for far less risqué yet equally intriguing reasons."

When Clara looked at her in question, her friend sighed, urged her to sit beside her on the bed, then took her hand.

"I think perhaps the time has come that we should be frank with one another," Maude said solemnly. "That we should finally just be blunt, however uncomfortable it might be. For friends should share, should they not? They should be honest and—"

"Maude?"

"Yes?"

"Just tell me what you wish to say." She stopped Maude's fan-dead flutter. "Straight to the point and without preamble."

"Yes, yes, quite right." Maude eyed Clara with cautious uncertainty. "As I suspect you know, your late husband frequented the Lyon's Den." She bit her lower lip and squeezed Clara's hand. "And for that, I am so very, very sorry, my dear, because..."

"He was there enjoying Mrs. Dove-Lyon's women when not with his mistress," she filled in when Maude trailed off. It had been one thing learning she was to marry him against her wishes, another to realize he was such a womanizer. She'd long past swallowed that bitter pill, though. Eventually, she was grateful for his lack of interest in her. "What does my late husband's behavior have to do with Lord Durham being there, though?"

"Well, if I gather things correctly," Maude replied, "through the brief unintended snippets Lord MacLauchlin may have let slip." She shook her head. "Not that I'm saying he did."

"Maude?"

"Yes."

"Out with it already!"

"Well, I'll *say*."

"I really wish you would."

"Fine." Maude fanned herself again. "If we are to skip all propriety and cut right to it, Lord Durham was never there to enjoy the dark pleasures of a woman but to learn what he could about you."

That same little thrill went through her again. "About me? Are you sure?"

"Yes." Maude shrugged a shoulder. "Plus a bit extra, if I understood my lord's random innuendoes about it."

"Might you be a tad more specific?" She held up a finger when Maude inhaled deeply, likely to go on at length. "Remember, straight to the point and without preamble."

"Straight to the point." Maude nodded. "All right then." She squeezed Clara's hand again. "From what I could ascertain, your lord has been, for lack of a better explanation, watching over you for several years."

"*Years?*" she whispered, unable to find her voice. "I don't understand."

"But I think you do." Maude looked at her with her heart in her eyes. "He never stopped loving you, madam. Not for a second."

"But he was married," she managed. "Had a family." She tried to grasp what Maude implied. "Do you mean to say he went there the whole time? His poor wife!"

"No, no." Maude shook her head. "I assure you, it was nothing like that. From what Lord MacLauchlin might or might not have hinted at, after your lord's wife had passed, he began investigating."

"Investigating?" she exclaimed. "Me?"

"Rumors *surrounding* you," Maude clarified, flinching when Clara's hand tightened around hers.

"*What* rumors?"

Maude's lips curled down, and sadness flickered in her eyes. "Must we?"

"Must we what?"

"Say the things we never said?"

Clara swallowed and looked away, suddenly understanding where Maude was going with this.

"My late husband was not the easiest man," she finally granted softly. "If that is what you are implying."

"It is, madam," Maude said just as softly, finally abandoning her fan to take Clara's hands in hers. "I know. I was there. He was...difficult. Better, I would say, when gone rather than at home."

No truer words were ever uttered.

Surrey had never hit her or her daughter, but he did abuse their servants. Hence Clara's maids not returning to Dowager Surrey, as

Maude had claimed their first night here. Instead, they went their own way lest risk employment by another man like Surrey. The best place for her late husband was always, without question, anywhere else. Quite frankly, out carousing or finding pleasure in another woman's bed was a Godsend.

"Yes, his absence was always best." Of the mind to end the conversation and take a stroll while Maude gave Mabel lessons, she stood and wrapped a shawl around her shoulders. "As I'm sure you understand, my late husband is no longer of concern to me."

What *was* of concern, however, was Isaac's behavior. About which she intended to speak with him. For, on top of everything else, it most certainly pointed toward his feelings for her never waning. She had hoped to speak with him at greater length last night, but clearly, that had not worked out.

"Very good, madam," Maude agreed. "Best Lord Surrey remain in the past." She tidied Clara's dress while she saw to the sashes of her bonnet. "Now it is time to look to the future." Yet back to the past, she went, determined, it seemed, that Clara got the whole story. "Honestly, though, it's a wonder Lord Durham did not visit Mrs. Dove-Lyon's sooner." She nodded once. "It speaks much to his character."

"For shame." She frowned. "He was married, Maude."

"As was your late husband." Implying it irrelevant to the conversation, Maude waved it away. "What I mean to say is…" Her brow creased, and she shook her head. "Never mind. It was improper for me to bring up to begin with. Whatever would Lord MacLauchlin think when I'm *sure* he let it slip in great confidence?"

"Quite right." Yet, as Maude had intended, Clara's curiosity was piqued. She sighed. "Just tell me already."

Maude's gaze turned innocent. "Tell you what?"

"Whatever Lord MacLauchlin said you feel I should know."

"Did I say all that, then?"

"You may as well have."

"I suppose, if you insist, though I should warn you, it's shameless and innocent gossip that may or may not be true." Maude's voice dropped to a near-whisper. "It seems Lady Durham did not love your lord. In fact, some say the only person she truly loved was herself."

"That *is* quite inappropriate of you to say." Clara frowned again. "And even more inappropriate to imply it gave him the right to frequent Mrs. Dove-Lyon's establishment sooner." She gave Maude a look. "I know you say such to let me know his heart might have always been mine, but still. Him loving another in the meantime would have made no difference. Rather I wish he had, for he deserved it."

"Yes, madam," Maude replied softly, properly chastised but at the same time resolute. "Whilst you have my most humble apologies, I said it more so you knew you shared a common bond all these years."

Her friend's gaze grew most serious, and she hesitated before continuing. "We will never speak of it again if that is your wish, but you must remember *your* history is *my* history. Though most certainly difficult for you and Lady Mabel with your late husband, it was just as difficult for me to watch." She squeezed Clara's hand again. "On that note, nothing would make me happier, and I believe our Lord MacLauchlin agrees, than to see you and Lord Durham rediscover the love you once shared. Mutual love you *both* deserve." Her cheeks warmed. "For it still burns brightly. Of that, there can be no doubt."

"Then let it come as it may," she murmured, content to leave it at that. Maude's heart was in the right place, but these were things Isaac should tell her when he was ready. Things that were his and his alone to divulge.

In the meantime, she must get him to open up to her more. To remain out of his self-imposed seclusion so that they might know each other again. Last night had been almost perfect. The way he had kissed her unforgettable. She had yearned for him to bring her upstairs. They had already been wedded to others, so the formalities of waiting until after marriage to consummate need not stand.

Yet, it had mattered naught in the end. Rather, in the brief jaunt inside, he'd withdrawn back into himself and set her aside, determined to keep her at arm's length once more. Had he understood what she'd said to him in regard to the fortune teller? Did he understand that the question that weighed most on her mind was if he still cared about her as much as she did him?

"What did you mean yesterday, Maude?" she asked impulsively but had to know. "What did you mean when you said Lord Durham brooded because of fanciful things?"

"Oh, I really should not have mentioned that."

Clara arched a brow. "Why, when you have mentioned everything else?"

"Well, some might think our lord silly for it." Maude shook her head, woeful. "And that does not seem right."

Isaac? Silly? That's the last word she would ever use to describe him. "I would never think Lord Durham silly."

"No, of course, you would not." Maude leaned closer. "It seems our lord fears his rotten luck. Even, as I'm told, that he might be cursed."

"Heavens," she murmured, frowning, yet she understood right away. "Because of his losses?"

"So it seems." Maude sighed. "Now he fears the same happening to you and Mabel."

"That's awful," she whispered, but it made perfect sense. Though Isaac had never been particularly superstitious, she could understand his hesitation. Especially if he still cared for her as much as she suspected he did. "I must speak with him."

How to lend him comfort, though? How to convince him everything would be okay? That he was not dooming them. What she discovered when Maude went in search of Mabel, and she wandered down to the gardens soon after, gave her an idea. She needed to remind him of the here and now—the vitality of his new family.

First, though, she would have to share a bit of their past.

Chapter Fourteen

Isaac wasn't sure what to make of Mabel flinging her arms around him or of the look on Clara's face when she rounded the corner, other than he suspected his heart was in more trouble than ever. Not only because of the affectionate hope in Clara's eyes but because of Mabel's embrace. Something he had not felt since his daughter had last hugged him.

"Good morning, Mother." Mabel smiled and curtsied. "My lord was just telling me wonderful love stories about his ancestors."

Clara's brows shot up. "Love stories?"

"Oh, yes," Mabel rambled on before he had a chance to respond. "Ones to rival your own, to be sure."

Bloody hell. This was spiraling out of control quickly.

Clara's brows edged even higher. Her voice cracked in surprise. "Our own?"

"Why, yes." Mabel's smile widened. "You know. How our lord rescued us, *you*, because he loves—"

"Ah, there you are," Maude exclaimed, coming around the corner just in the nick of time. She glanced from Clara to Isaac, no doubt sensing she had walked into something. "It's time to resume lessons, Lady Mabel."

Mabel pouted before looking at Clara and Isaac with hope. "Must I, when it is such a beautiful day for a stroll?"

"I'm afraid so," he replied. Though normally he would have enjoyed her company, he feared what Mabel might say next. The truths she seemed intent to reveal.

"I agree with my lord," Clara concurred, not seeming distressed in the least that he had stepped in. "Lessons must come first."

"Indeed." Maude shooed Mabel along. "There will be plenty of time for a stroll later."

He was about to excuse himself as well when Clara begged a moment of his time. "Might you walk with me, my lord?" Her gaze flickered to the woodland. "I seem to remember a beautiful stream down that way."

Hell and damnation, it would be rude to say no.

He clasped his hands behind his back to keep from reeling her close and picking up where they left off last night. "But of course, madam."

"Let me begin by thanking you for the lovely garments and jewelry." She seemed to weigh her words as they strolled. "They were...too much."

They were not nearly enough. Not when it came to her.

"My pleasure." And just so the extravagance made sense. "You will soon be the Marchioness of Durham, after all."

It mattered naught that she was already a duchess with plenty of her own clothing nor that she came with substantial wealth. He wanted her to have things from him.

"They are truly lovely," she replied graciously. They made their way down the quaint and winding woodland path. "And fit so very perfectly. Almost too perfectly, some might say given the long years in between us seeing one another."

Ah, the real reason for their mid-morning stroll. He tensed but remained outwardly calm. Unfazed when, in truth, he worried over how much she knew.

"I heard rumor you had changed little," he replied smoothly.

"Do they talk about me that much at the Lyon's Den, then?"

"You would be amazed what is said in those places."

"I can just imagine." She handed him a slip of paper. "If, that is, they had been the ones to share such."

He cursed under his breath, noting the date. While he could just as easily lie his way out of this, something about the watchful look in her lovely eyes kept him truthful.

"Allow me to explain."

"I wish you would."

They stopped at the stream's edge. Overgrown with old trees and moss-covered rocks, he had always thought the spot peaceful.

"My explanation goes back a tad further than the Lyon's Den," he began.

"I imagined it would."

"Back to when you married the Duke of Surrey."

When he hesitated, wondering if he should confess to so much, she murmured, "Go on. Please."

He paused a moment longer before he nodded. It was time, and he wasn't entirely sure why. Perhaps because of what Blake had said about Clara having been in Isaac's heart for so long, or maybe because of how he'd just felt when Mabel hugged him. How eager he was for a new beginning. Either way, it was time to reveal how he had felt years ago. Not because he felt cornered but simply because he wanted to.

Despite his fears, it suddenly seemed crucial.

He wanted Clara to understand.

"In the end, even though I was under the impression you no longer wanted to see me, I blamed myself for not trying harder," he said softly. "I should never have given up. Not for a moment. Not when I cared so deeply. Especially when I heard what kind of man Lord Surrey was."

He shook his head and gathered his thoughts before continuing, trying to keep things logical rather than show too much emotion. "So yes, both before and after my wife died, I kept tabs on you, Clara. Watched you from afar the best I could." He clenched his jaw, trying to keep fury at bay. "Oftentimes," *all the time,* "I wished I could intercede sooner when I knew your situation with Surrey was less than favorable." He shrugged a shoulder, getting back on point. "So it's safe to say, after keeping an eye on you for a time, knowing your dress size was to be expected."

She swallowed hard and stared at him as if digesting everything he had said. Though hesitation flared in her eyes, she didn't seem overly surprised he knew of Surrey's reputation. While she could have mentioned Isaac watching over her these past years, she instead focused on how much he might have understood at the beginning.

"Did you know what kind of man my late husband was before we married?" she asked.

"Of course not."

"Then you need not be sorry." She released a shaky sigh. "Even then, I doubt you could have dissuaded my father." Her sad gaze drifted to the shimmering water. "I suppose it could be said I did not fight hard enough either. Having suspected you intended to propose, I might have sought you out to see if we…"

Clara trailed off a moment, clearly rallying her emotions, her honesty humbling when it came. "Truth told, I considered seeking you out, but self-doubt got in the way. Then fear that perhaps I would be asking too much of you." She shook her head. "Perhaps I was wrong thinking you wished to marry me. And if I were not, and you were willing, if we married in secret without my father's permission, what might that do to your reputation? Your family's good name?"

"I would not have cared," he replied more passionately than intended. But he meant it. "You should know I tried to get your father's permission, Clara, but he put me off only to grant it to Surrey." He sighed. "So even if I had worked up the courage to ask you sooner, it wouldn't have mattered. He had already made up his mind."

"I should have known." Pained, she closed her eyes before she opened them again and looked at him. "Why hesitate in asking me to begin with, though? You *had* to know you were the only one for me, Isaac?"

"Looking back, I would say it was fear that for some unknown reason, you might have said no." He scowled, wishing he could reach back in time and do things differently. Be more courageous. Forward. Reckless, if need be. Anything to ensure she remained by his side. "On top of that, I still didn't have your father's permission, which, I'll admit, rattled me."

"I imagine it would." Her eyes softened with resolve. "However unfortunate, I suppose it no longer matters. What *does* matter is the here and now." She looked at him curiously. "How we feel now. How *you* feel."

Eager. Hopeful. So in love, it hurt.

Yet still, first and foremost, fearful.

"I feel...tentative."

"I gathered." She cocked her head, perplexed. "Why, though, when your actions of late betray you? While it might be wishful thinking and forgive my forthrightness, but I get the impression you still care a great deal for me." She searched his eyes. "Yet you continue suffering some great inner conflict."

While he had confessed a great deal thus far, was he ready to share that much truth? To break down the last barrier that might stand between them?

"You need not share yet, my lord," Clara murmured, clearly sensing his hesitation. Her concerned gaze never left him. "Though I hope in time, it might be like it once was between us. That you might

112

be more open and keep sharing rather than let the year go by being so distanced from me."

How he wanted to finger one of her vibrant curls. Reel her into his arms. Tell her that he had never loved another as much as he did her. But he hesitated, still fearful despite all good reason.

"I have, as I suspect you know," Clara went on, "become a very patient sort, thanks to my late husband. So I do not mind waiting."

They started back up the path, her next revelation, without doubt, said on purpose. Moreover, hinting at just how much she knew. The real reason he kept her at arm's length.

The last barrier between them.

"Did you know my daughter and I were sick a few years back?"

"I did not." He frowned, startled that he hadn't heard about that. But then it made sense that Surrey didn't find it relevant enough to talk about when gambling. "I'm sorry to hear that."

"Thank you." She glanced at him with relief. "I will admit it was terrifying to see Mabel so ill, but fortunately, she and I are remarkably resilient."

"That is good news, indeed."

And a direct message that he need not fear them dying on him.

"It is, *was*, good news," she said softly. "There can be no doubt she is a strong little girl."

"I would hope," he murmured before he could stop himself.

"There is no need to hope." Clara stopped and rested her hand on his arm, pain once again in her curious gaze. "That's it, is it not? The reason for your evasiveness and hesitation? Why you have avoided us these past few weeks? You fear losing us, as you lost your family?"

"Is that not a valid fear?"

"It is." Her brows pulled together. "But it should not stop you from caring, my lord. It shouldn't keep you from finding happiness again if you think such is possible with Mabel and me."

"This has nothing to do with my happiness." He continued walking before he lost himself in her gaze. "But rather, your safety. Especially considering…"

When he trailed off, she prompted him to continue. "Considering what?"

"It does not matter." He shook his head. "Not anymore."

"Clearly, it does." She frowned. "Considering what, my lord?"

"Isaac," he muttered.

"Isaac," she agreed. "Please just tell me so that I might understand."

"I should not."

"But I wish you would."

"Yet I will not because—"

"Just tell me," she exclaimed. "Tell me as you once would have when we kept nothing from each other. When you would have spoken without hesitation because I was your dearest friend."

"Which is why your safety must come first," he bit out, sighing at his frankness. But there it was. He met her gaze. "How could I, in good conscience, risk you and your daughter's safety when you have already been at risk for years?" Then blunter still, he gave her all of it. "Because getting close to me could very well renew that risk all over again."

She frowned, focusing on the first part of what he had said. "You thought us in that much danger with my late husband?"

"I had no sure way of knowing, but yes, I feared it." She might have escaped Surrey unscathed, but it was only a matter of time with a man like that.

"Perhaps I did, too," Clara whispered before clearing her throat. Instead of delving deeper into what life had been like with Surrey, she focused on Isaac's past. "That's the reason for your hesitation, then?" Her brows creased when she looked at him. "Because you think everyone close to you dies?"

114

"Do they not?"

"No." Clara shook her head. "No, they do not." She stopped, rested her hand on his arm again, and looked at him with fresh compassion. "You have been close to Lord MacLauchlin your whole life, and he is alive and well, is he not?" Before he could respond, she went on. "Not just that, but what of Mabel and I? You try to keep us at a distance, yet I would hazard to guess you have kept Mabel close in your own way since she was born, and we've been close since we were children." She gestured at herself. "Yet here we are, perfectly healthy."

He had never looked at it like that, but she was right.

The moment he knew what kind of man Surrey was and started keeping an eye on him, he'd kept Mabel in his thoughts. As to Clara, she had always been in his heart, closer to him than most.

"Your Grace." Laurence appeared just ahead, pulling them from their conversation. His butler bowed to Clara, then to Isaac. "My lord." He held out a little silver tray with a missive on it, his gaze distressed. "You will want to read this straight away, Lord Durham. For it seems a problem has arisen."

115

Chapter Fifteen

Isaac's expression darkened as he read the message Laurence had just delivered.

"What is it?" Clara looked from his butler to him. "What does it say?"

When Isaac shook his head as though he were not going to share, she repeated herself.

"It seems one of our marital banns has been contested." Fury flashed in Isaac's eyes. "And I have no one to blame but myself for posting them to begin with." He looked at Laurence. "See a carriage made ready. I will be going into town post-haste." His attention returned to Clara. "I bid you good day, madam."

When he bowed and strode for the castle, she pursued. "I will go with you."

"You will not."

"I most certainly will." She moved a bit faster when he didn't slow down. "This is my union, too, my lord. So, I have every right to confront those who take issue with my upcoming matrimony."

"You will not be going anywhere near Kent," he muttered, gesturing that Blake stop when they caught sight of him ahead.

"Lord Kent?" Her heart slammed into her throat. "But I thought him out of the country?"

"As did I." Isaac gave Blake a look when they joined him. "It seems Kent not only returned from business early, if he was ever really out of the country, but has opted to ignore my challenge."

Blake scanned the letter and cursed under his breath.

"What challenge?" Heavens above, what was this all about? "Please tell me you didn't do anything foolish." She narrowed her eyes, coming to the only conclusion she could based on the word *challenge*. Isaac had invited Lord Kent to a duel. "Tell me you did not do what my late husband did, for *surely* you are wiser than that, my lord?"

"I kept things on my terms and off property, away from you and your daughter." Isaac shouldered into a cloak. "Best that lout be dealt with once and for all."

"Or," she grew more fearful by the moment, "he deals with *you* once and for all."

"I'm an excellent shot," he countered. "So you need not worry."

"So was my late husband," she cared not for good manners at this point, "yet he lies in his grave!" Her voice wobbled. "Somewhere, I refuse to see you now that we finally have a chance. Somewhere, I wouldn't want to see you either way!"

Despite his aggravation at Kent's audacity, Blake's brows perked at the implication she and Isaac were making headway together. "She makes a good point, cousin."

"Point or no," Isaac grumbled, "it seems Kent has other intentions anyway." He shook his head at Clara when Blake helped her on with her jacket. "You are *not* going with me. Kent is far too unpredictable. My cousin will accompany me instead."

"I most certainly am going with you, and I will give you two very good reasons why," she replied. "First, we are better equipped to counter-argue together than apart with those who contest our marriage." She glanced from Blake to upstairs then back to Isaac. "Secondly, you are right about Kent's instability. That in mind, I

117

would prefer someone who knows how to shoot a gun staying to protect my daughter and Miss Maude." She arched a brow at Isaac. "Surely, you see the good sense in that, my lord."

He went to respond but stopped, started again, then snapped his mouth shut in frustration.

"Fine." He headed out the door Laurence held open and grumbled over his shoulder, "Let's get to town, then."

Minutes later, all of which Isaac paced and fumed, the carriage came around, and they were off.

"So, should we assume this has to do with my late husband promising me to Lord Kent?" How she wished she and Isaac were already married. Something she knew better than to bring up at the moment. "Surely, such a wayward agreement cannot stand?"

"It will stand over my dead body," Isaac ground out.

"Which is still a distinct possibility," she reminded, terrified to think it. "Why, again, did you challenge him to begin with?"

"Because he thought to kill your husband and make you his," he spat, quite blunt. "Though, in truth, I should have challenged him earlier for all the trouble he caused you and Surrey, no matter how little I liked your late husband."

"You knew so much then?" she murmured, still reeling from what he had shared earlier. How closely he had followed her late husband and, in turn, her. She had purposely held back what she'd learned from Maude. That she already knew much of what he had divulged. Not only because she'd hoped he would share of his own accord but because she didn't want to get Blake in trouble.

For surely, like Maude, he was playing at a bit of matchmaking.

Truth be told, their nudging was probably for the best, all things considered. For, she and Isaac were, at last, starting to communicate as they should. It infuriated Clara that her father had denied him all those years ago, but at least now she knew the truth. Not only had he not given up on them, but he'd tried to go about things correctly

118

from the start. Blast her father for his meddlesome, self-righteous ways. Moreover, that she had ever let him have so much control over her life.

"I knew enough about your late husband," Isaac replied, drawing her back to the present, keeping with the truth now. "I gambled with him over the years so that I might better know his character." His gaze leveled with her. "More pointedly, as I implied earlier, so that I might know his wife was well-cared for."

"And your conclusion?"

"That you were not." His expression darkened before he finally asked what she knew he had been longing to ask. "Did he hurt you, Clara? Did he hurt Mabel?"

"No, not us." She shook her head. "Not physically, anyway."

His shoulders slumped ever-so-slightly in relief before he tensed again. "He had a sharp tongue, though, yes?"

"To say the least." She gazed out the window and gathered herself, not wanting to upset Isaac any more than he already was but at the same time comfortable with him. Feeling that same easy connection they had always shared. "He was a petty man. Though I wouldn't wish death on anyone, I will admit to being thankful not just Mabel and I are away from him, but the servants. He did not make things easy for them."

"That is unfortunate, and I'm sorry for it." Isaac placed his hand over hers. "I imagine that was not easy on any of you, especially Mabel being so young."

"No." She shook her head. "But Maude and I did well to keep her sheltered from it. Mabel might have occasionally heard his rantings, but mostly she just suffered an absent father. As it was, his disdain of her kept him away."

"Bloody fool," Isaac muttered, apologizing for his language. His jaw tightened. A vein ticked in his temple. "I would have done anything to be in his position. To spend time with my daughter…"

119

When he trailed off, she threaded her fingers with his and looked at him. "And that is why you will make a much better father to Mabel than he ever would. You already have been better, doing far more for her than he ever did."

Isaac paused several long moments, digesting that, and more it seemed, based on what he asked next.

"Did you want more?" he finally asked softly, surprising her considering his reservations. His fear of losing loved ones. "Do you still want more?"

"Children?"

"Yes."

"I would have said no had you asked me a year ago, if for no other reason than their upbringing." She squeezed his hand. "But now? Yes, absolutely. And you?"

Though fleeting, fear flashed in his eyes before he looked out the window again. "It is hard to imagine."

She didn't fault him that, given what he'd suffered. Rather than continue the conversation, she respected the moment and let the matter rest. Yet with the fear she had glimpsed in his eyes, she also saw a flash of hope—an unmistakable flicker of longing.

Instead of stopping at the registry this time, they went straight to Isaac's local parish, where his minister had already read their banns three times. The last was read just yesterday, which would have been the third Sunday since they were posted.

"My Lord Marquess and Your Grace," the minister said grimly, bowing when they entered. "Many thanks for coming so swiftly, for I fear our visitor would not have left my office otherwise." He sighed and gestured that they join him. "Come, let us see if we can resolve this matter."

The matter, as they knew it would be, was Lord Kent. A tall, thin man with a hawk-like nose and shifty eyes, Kent notched his chin when they entered. "About time." He bowed to her, his gaze a bit too appreciative to be considered polite. "Duchess Surrey." His attention narrowed on Isaac. "Lord Durham."

"Lord Kent," Isaac replied curtly when the minister urged them to sit. "I see you chose to ignore my challenge."

"Yes." A grin slithered onto Kent's face when he looked her way again. "But then why risk my life when there is still so much pleasure to be found in it?"

Isaac scowled. "You do understand you speak to my future wife?"

"You mean *my* future wife." Kent looked at the minister with impatience. "If you would?"

The minister handed Isaac a missive with an official-looking seal on it. She chilled at the familiar emblem.

Isaac's features grew more and more thunderous as he read it. "Good God, man." His eyes rounded on Kent. "What kind of monster are you?"

"Oh, dear, do not take the good Lord's name in vain, if you will," the minister pleaded. He wrung his hands and glanced between the men. "I do beg of you both to respect our house of worship."

"But of course." Isaac stood. "Let us take our disagreement outside, Kent." He tapped the letter. "For *this* will not stand."

"But it will, Durham." Kent grinned. "So says the Archbishop of Canterbury."

"What is it?" Clara took the letter and read it, chilled all the more at its near medieval context. "Surely *not!*"

Potential witnesses to a drunken pre-duel agreement were one thing, this document quite another. It had been signed not only by her late husband and Kent but by the bishop himself, confirming the rumors true. She was to be Lord Kent's wife in the event that Lord Surrey lost his life in their duel.

"This will not stand," Isaac grunted. "Come on, Kent. Outside so that we might settle this like gentlemen."

"On the other end of your gun barrel?" Kent snorted. "I think not." He turned his smug look on the minister. "Is this not a viable reason to deny the marriage between Lord Durham and Duchess Surrey?" He gestured at the letter. "As you can plainly see, her late husband and I signed an agreement that was verified by the archbishop."

"Which I dare say is rather disturbing all things considered." The minister looked at Clara kindly. "Unless that is, you were in agreement, Your Grace."

"I most certainly was not." She scowled at Kent. "I cannot begin to understand what you and my late husband were thinking, but I will *not* marry you." She rounded her eyes. "Even if the archbishop approved it."

"By law, Duchess," shadows darkened Kent's eyes, "you will."

Isaac frowned at the minister. "This positively reeks of wife-selling, and well you know it. Even then, the ridiculous centuries-old custom was a *mutual* way around illegally divorcing." He gestured with disgust at the letter. "The archbishop would never agree to such. Especially without Her Grace's approval. Therefore, I call into account the validity of this document."

"So, you think it a forgery?"

"I do."

"Then, we must investigate."

"I agree."

"I do not." Lord Kent's eyes widened on the minister. "You dare doubt my word or that of our good archbishop?"

"I am simply doing my due diligence to see all parties well satisfied." The minister glanced at Isaac and Clara remorsefully. "To that end, I'm afraid your marriage must be put on hold until I have discussed this matter with the archbishop."

"Well, I'll be," Kent huffed, standing. "I am most offended."

"And for that, I apologize, my lord." The minister stood as well. "I will send a messenger straight away to the Archbishop of Canterbury. Until then, we have a lovely little inn for you and yours to enjoy."

"A lovely little inn?" Kent mouthed as though the suggestion tasted bad on his tongue. His sly gaze slid Clara's way. "But then I suppose if Duchess Surrey is in town as well, all is tolerable."

"She will not be in town," Isaac said through clenched teeth. "But remaining at my residence until I receive proof from the archbishop. Then, because I'm law-abiding to a fault, we will go from there."

Everyone glanced at Isaac in surprise. Why did that sound like he might, after the frustration he'd just shown, allow this to happen?

The minister's bushy brows shot up. "So you will agree to this if we receive word from the archbishop that all is on the up and up, Lord Durham?"

"What choice do I have?" Isaac relented. "In return, I ask for your blessing that Duchess Surrey and her young daughter remain under my care. It's enough the child's life was so upended coming here. Might we keep things stable for her a few days longer?"

"Yes, I do agree." The minister nodded. "Until this matter is resolved, I will see that the constable understands the arrangement."

Isaac nodded his thanks, and Kent grumbled in dismay.

Though grateful she and Mabel would not have to stay in town, Clara could barely think straight as they got back into the carriage a few minutes later. Though she tried questioning Isaac about his possible change of heart, he remained vague and relatively tight-lipped. Which, naturally, got her thinking how conveniently this might have worked out for him in the end.

For, despite everything that had happened between her arrival at his estate and now, the fact remained, to the best of her knowledge, that Isaac didn't want to be married.

123

So this might just be the perfect way out of it.

Chapter Sixteen

"It was bloody wise of me not to bring my pistol," Isaac muttered to Blake later that evening. They waited in front of the fire, not just for Clara, Maude, and Mabel but new arrivals. "I would have shot Kent point-blank and been done with it."

"And done with your good name and freedom, too," Blake reminded. "But it matters naught because you did the right thing."

"I can only hope." His nerves were strung tight. "You have no idea how hard it was to rein in my anger. To see reason in the midst of such…" What were the words? "Shadiness. Deceptiveness. Utter lawlessness!"

The ride back to the castle with Clara had been pure torture. He had wanted to explain his change of attitude but couldn't. Not yet. Instead, he had conceded he'd been a fool not getting a common license to begin with and reiterated why he must respect the laws of the land and entertain Kent's claim.

There was no missing the sadness in her eyes when she asked why he seemed so angry one moment, then accepting the next. Though he remained evasive, her takeaway, as it had to be until he knew who would play along with his scheme, was that he saw this as a means out of their marriage.

"Yet you kept a clear mind and saw reason despite how upset you were with Kent." Blake clapped Isaac on the shoulder and eyed his pocket. "Are you sure you are up to this, old friend?" His grin blossomed into a smile. "I dare say, I truly hope you are."

"I am." Despite his reservations about Clara and Mabel's future with him, he was never so sure of anything. "All the cards are in play."

"Well, then, tonight should be one for the MacLauchlin history books." Blake raised his glass to the Scotsmen staring down at them. "May we do our ancestors proud."

He tipped his glass to a painting hidden in the shadows. A more piratical MacLauchlin watching him with a curious eye, wondering just how far he was willing to go. "Best we toast to the correct ancestor at that, cousin."

Blake chuckled. "Very true."

They had no sooner taken a sip when the others joined them. Maude looked fetching in a light blue dress; little Mabel, pretty in pink; and Clara, stunning in one of the gowns he'd had made for her. The crème-colored silk dress had a rose-trimmed neckline that accentuated the soft mounds of her cleavage with tiny matching roses along the waistline and sleeves.

Bows and curtsies were exchanged before he urged everyone to sit, and drinks were served.

"Is this not a touch early for dinner?" Maude blushed when Blake's lips lingered overly long on the back of her hand when he kissed it.

"There are things that must be seen to first," Blake explained.

"What sorts of things?" Mabel asked.

Before he had a chance to answer, Laurence appeared at the door and addressed Isaac. "They have arrived, my lord."

"Very good."

He stood and held out his elbow to Clara. "Might you accompany me, Your Grace?"

She glanced from the others to him. "Just me?"

126

"Yes, just you."

When Maude sat beside Mabel and nodded all was well, Clara slipped her arm into Isaac's and looked at him curiously. "Where might we be off to?"

"Not far," he assured, leading her down the hallway.

Back to where it all began.

"I do not understand." Her voice wobbled. "You need not take me aside to tell me what you truly want, for I gathered it in the ministry earlier...then on the ride back here."

"What matters most right now, madam," he said softly, "is what *you* want."

Confusion lit her gaze. "I believe I made that perfectly clear when I sought out Mrs. Dove-Lyon."

"You made clear you were running from a madman, which was confirmed today." Isaac stopped and fingered a tendril of her hair. "What I'm asking is, are you sure you wish to marry me?" He shook his head. "I will protect you, either way, Clara."

She considered him for a moment, understanding what he really asked. "You mean, do I wish to marry you and risk my life? Mabel's? Because you fear everyone you love dies though I made it clear they do not."

"Yes." She had no idea how much those words had meant. How they had gotten through to him. Made him see things differently. "To put it so bluntly."

"Of course, I still wish to marry you, Isaac." Clara shook her head. "Not just for protection but because I believe the three of us would be happy." She rested her hand on his chest. Her gaze never left his face. "If I thought marrying you was a risk, I would not be here. Nor would Mabel, because her safety is of the utmost importance to me."

Though he struggled because he knew how real this might become, *would* become, he had no choice but to push forward. Not just for obvious reasons but because of what he felt in his heart.

What he had always felt.

Would always feel.

They continued walking. "Then let us see to business."

"I don't understand." She frowned. "What sort of business?"

Rather than respond, he thanked Laurence when he opened the door to the piano room. As requested, all awaited them, including the minister, magistrate, constable, Lord Kent, and one other.

"What is the meaning of this?" Kent scowled and stood. "Why was I summoned here?" The earl gestured at the constable in case Isaac got any ideas. "With protection, I might add." He glanced from Clara to Isaac. "Have you decided it best Duchess Surrey stay in town after all? For you might have just—"

"Sit, Lord Kent." Isaac gestured at the servant waiting to top off Kent's expensive brandy. "Sit so that we might talk about something more important."

"What could *possibly* be more important?" Yet Kent sat, nodding with haughty approval at the refill and expensive cigar handed to him.

"I wish to discuss something you might have heard a rumor about." Isaac nodded at Laurence to proceed. "Something you might find very important."

Kent's brows perked. "Is that so?"

"It is."

When Laurence bowed to Kent, he then opened a sizeable velvet box, everyone gasped at its contents.

"Devil's teeth," Kent murmured in awe. His eyes widened on the large shimmering ruby inside. "Is that what I think it is?"

"The infamous jewel bestowed upon my family by King Edward III, himself, over four hundred and fifty years ago?" Isaac asked. "Why, yes, it is."

Kent licked his lips and went to touch it, only for the extra person in the room to step forward. "You best not, my lord."

Kent's brows snapped together. "And who are you again?"

"The town jeweler, my lord." The man's reverent gaze never left the gem. He pulled out a magnifying glass. "I beg of you, let me examine it first. For if it is the real thing, something as simple as the oil from your hand could diminish its value."

"What does a jeweler from a small town like this know of something so," Kent's eyes remained glued to the gem, "spectacular?"

"Assuming it *is* spectacular." The jeweler eyed the ruby with uncertainty. "It could just as easily be a fake."

"And he would know." The magistrate rocked back on his heels and nodded with assurance at Kent. "He worked for Foxhills, so his credentials are impeccable. He can spot a forgery easily but would need a closer look."

"Foxhills, you say?" Kent murmured.

"Oh, yes, we even did work for King George III," the jeweler replied.

"Is that right?"

"Yes, my lord." The jeweler glanced at Isaac in question. "I mean no ill-will, but might I take a closer look at it, Lord Dunham?"

"Of course."

"Very good, my lord. Thank you." The jeweler put on gloves, lifted the gem out gingerly, brought it to the candlelight, and studied it beneath his magnifying glass. "Oh, yes, *very* nice." He nodded and held it with great care at another angle. "My goodness, quite, *quite* nice." He turned it yet again, paused, and narrowed an eye. "Saints *above!*"

"What is it?" Kent waited with bated breath. "Did you find a flaw? An imperfection?" When the jeweler didn't answer, Kent grew exasperated. "Good God, man, what do you see!"

"The likes of which I have never seen," the jeweler whispered, renewed reverence in his overly large eye thanks to the glass he peered through. "Absolute…"

"Absolute *what*?" Kent snapped when the jeweler seemed tongue-tied with mystification.

"I'm so sorry, my lord." The jeweler blinked as if coming out of a stunned reverie and carefully placed the jewel back in its box. "I have never seen such a flawless gem. One so…" He struggled to find the words. His hands trembled when he pulled away as if the impact of what he'd just held finally hit him. "So very *stunningly* perfect. Beyond comparison." His gaze went to Kent. "Utterly ageless, if you will."

Wide-eyed, Kent looked from the jeweler to the ruby before it occurred to him; he had no idea why it had been brought out. Nor why the jeweler was present to appraise it.

"What is this about, Durham?" He scowled at Isaac. "Why are you showing me this?"

"Because I hope to strike a bargain."

"What sort of bargain?"

"Well, as you might have surmised earlier," Isaac replied woefully, "it became abundantly clear to me that you might just have a legitimate claim on Duchess Surrey."

He pressed his lips together and paused as though coming to terms with things.

"It just so happens," Isaac continued as if finally relenting, "that I applied for a special license when I married my late wife, so I know your document is not a forgery." He nodded once at Kent, acknowledging that he was right. "The archbishop's signature is, in fact, *very* much authentic, for I have seen it first-hand." He shook his head and clenched his hands, sure to look both frustrated and resolute. "So you see, I became torn between seeing through my dear late father's wishes and abiding by the law."

Kent frowned yet seemed mildly intrigued. "And what were your father's wishes?"

"That Duchess Surrey be well cared for." Isaac's gaze went to Clara. "As it was, she once meant a great deal to him. So much that he made me promise she would be taken care of no matter what." He sighed and looked at Kent. "So I suppose I must ask…will you let this go and allow me to see through my late father's wishes?" His reluctant gaze went to the gem. "Or will it take…more encouragement?"

Much to her credit, Clara remained expressionless through the whole spiel with her hands folded neatly on her lap. A façade she had undoubtedly perfected with Surrey.

"You would give up your family treasure for her?" Kent stuttered. "A mere woman?"

"I would give it up to honor my father's wishes," he corrected, fully aware Kent and his own father were close, so this was the best way to appeal to him. "Surely you understand, for nothing defines a man's honor more."

Kent eyed Isaac for a moment, evidently seeing what he was looking for in his steady gaze, before he nodded in agreement, then shook his head. "No, it does not." When his hungry attention returned to the gem and his fingers twitched with impatience, the jeweler handed him his gloves. "If you would prefer a closer look?"

"Most certainly." Kent snatched the gloves and yanked them on before he carefully lifted the gem. "Saints be, it has some weight to it, does it not?"

"Naturally." Isaac notched his chin, sure to sound properly snobbish. "It *did* belong to my distant relative, the King of England, after all."

"*Indeed.*" Kent brought it closer to the candlelight, and his jaw dropped. "What would you say it was worth?"

The jeweler apologized to the others that such a number should not be said aloud lest servants overhear, then whispered it in Kent's ear.

"Devil's cock," he exclaimed before apologizing absently for his foul language. His eyes rounded at the jeweler. "*Truly?*"

"Oh, yes." The man nodded avidly, his gaze rarely leaving the gem. "*Easily.*"

"I see." Kent cleared his throat and returned the gem to its case as though walking on thin ice. As if dropping it would be the end-all.

Would he give Isaac the answer he hoped for?

Or was this all for naught?

Soon   enough,   he   found   out.

Chapter Seventeen

Clara had no idea what to think of the masquerade she witnessed in Isaac's piano room other than it had been well-planned. While she knew for certain the tale he spun about his father was false, what of the gem? He had spoken of it little when they were young, sometimes claiming it a myth, other times, that it financed this estate.

No matter what came of it, she could say with relief that Isaac did not want her in Kent's grasp. Nor, based on what he'd said before they entered the room, did he want her to leave.

Rather, he seemed eager in a way he hadn't been up to this point.

"Sign this agreement that you release Duchess Surrey from the contract her late husband made on her behalf." Isaac set a quill, ink, and sheet of paper down in front of Lord Kent. "And I will relinquish my family gem to you." He set an ancient-looking framed document beside the ruby. "But first, read this carefully, for this authenticates the jewel and is in—"

"Hell and damnation, is that *his* signature?" Kent snagged the jeweler's magnifying glass and focused on the scrawl at the bottom of the document. "Is that King Edward III's actual *signature*?"

"Yes, it is."

"Stunning," Kent whispered, peering at it. "Absolutely *stunning.*"

"Sign the document," Isaac dipped the quill in ink, then put it in Kent's hand, "and both the gem and its authentication is yours."

Clara's pulse fluttered like mad, and her throat went bone dry.

Would he do it?

Dare she hope?

"Yes, yes, of course," Kent said dismissively, signing it without barely looking.

"Very good." Isaac handed her the document next, then the magistrate and minister for their signatures as well. "The gem now belongs to you, Lord Kent."

"Excellent." Kent shooed Laurence away when he went to close the box. "Then, I really must be off."

"Us, as well." The magistrate ushered Kent out, followed swiftly by the constable, minister, and jeweler. Laurence smiled and nodded before he closed the door, leaving Isaac and Clara alone.

"What just happened?" Confused and relieved but also breathless and excited, she looked at Isaac. "For, that all seemed quite…"

"Rushed? Final?" Isaac led her to the piano and urged her to sit. "Because it was. That chapter of your life and Lord Kent are part of your past now, Clara." He sank to his knee and pulled a ruby ring out of his pocket. "As to your future," he held it out to her, "that's as much in your hands now as it was the moment you sought out Mrs. Dove-Lyon."

She could barely breathe. Barely gather her thoughts.

"Only this time, I wish to go about things properly," Isaac continued. He held her hand and gazed at her like he once had. "As I meant to ask you in this very spot years ago, will you marry me, Clara?"

Emotions bubbled up. This was not a mere formality. He was serious.

"You want this?" she whispered, teary despite herself. "Truly?"

"I want you," he said without hesitation and with startling honesty. "So, yes, though fearful, I want to marry you, my love. As I believe I mentioned the very first night we met, I wish you to be my wife." His gaze flickered from the ring to her face. "The question remains, however, do you still want me?"

"You know, I do." She cupped his cheek. "But not at a distance as you initially stipulated. I want you here, with me, so that we might learn about one another again." Her voice dropped to a whisper. "Love one another."

"Yes," he murmured, sliding the ring onto her finger.

There were still things to understand. What had just happened with Lord Kent and the MacLauchlin jewel? But before she could utter another word, Isaac sat, pulled her against him, and closed his lips over hers. With that, any questions she might have had melted away. Instead, all that existed when he deepened their kiss was the same passion she had so feverishly felt in the maze yesterday.

"Play for me again," he murmured against her lips. "Or I might not last."

She smiled, understanding. Now was not the time to lose themselves to desire or even ask questions that didn't belong in the moment.

Now was for them.

This.

Right here. Right now.

"What shall I play?" she asked.

"Whatever you like." His gaze lingered on her face. "Whatever you feel."

"I don't think there's melody enough," she said softly but would give him what she could.

What she felt.

What she hoped for and needed.

Resting her fingers on the keys, she closed her eyes and let her emotions take over. She thought about the past few weeks and what had brought them to this moment. The sweet anticipation of seeing him again. The heartache that he might turn her away. The sadness she felt for his suffering, then the joy of seeing him smile at Mabel. At the way hope flickered in his gaze that he might rediscover what was lost to him.

Again, she had no idea she played until she opened her eyes, and the others had rejoined them. Mabel, Blake, and Maude. Even the minister and servants hovered on the outskirts as her fingers flew over the keys. This time the music was less somber and more hopeful, joyful even, the notes bringing a smile to all, whether it be one of nostalgia or happiness.

"That was so very, very lovely, Mother," Mabel praised when the last note floated off. "I did not know you could play the pianoforte."

"Yes, darling." She took her daughter's hand, for the first time in a long time, looking forward to what lay ahead. "I'm so glad you know now. I shall have to play for you more often."

"I would like that." Mabel eyed the keys with wonder. "Might you teach me how to play?"

"I would like nothing more." She patted the seat next to her. "Would you like to tap a key or two now?"

"Oh, yes," she gushed before Maude cleared her throat, clearly reminding her of something. Mabel smiled and urged Clara to stand. "But first, we must see to things."

"Things?" She met her daughter's smile. "What sort of things?"

Though she tried, Mabel abandoned all decorum and tugged Clara after her. "*Wondrous* things, Mother. Truly wondrous."

She was led all the way outside with everyone following until they reached the torch-lit maze, and Isaac's hand replaced Mabel's.

She smiled at him. "What is this?"

136

He smiled in return. "Come, let us find out."

They walked beneath floral archways highlighted by torchlight until they arrived at her sculpture. Isaac took a ring of flowers off its head and placed it on hers before his gaze returned to her face. "I thought perhaps this would be the perfect spot to exchange our vows. Of course, if you would prefer a chapel, we could—"

Clara put a finger to his lips and shook her head. She looked from Mabel to him and smiled. "I think this is perfect."

"Very good, madam," the minister said, stepping forward without preamble.

At long last, vows were finally said. Promises she feared she and Isaac might never exchange. Yet here they were, rolling back the clock, losing themselves in each other's eyes as swiftly as they once did. Yes, fear was still there in his steady gaze, but it was a fear she was determined to conquer. To prove had no place in what they would share.

"I now pronounce you man and wife," the minister finally announced. "You may kiss the bride."

Isaac cupped her cheeks and did just that, his kiss hungry but tempered due to their audience.

"How perfectly lovely," Mabel gushed, wrapping her arms around them before they had a chance to pull apart.

"Good gracious, child," Maude chastised but wore an equally dreamy smile when congratulating them, then embracing Clara.

Blake followed suit, congratulating them both. "Might we go in and warm up, then?" He grinned. "Perhaps celebrate how well this went?"

"To be sure," the minister agreed. "But first, let us go get things signed and make this legal before, well," he ushered them along, "let's just get paperwork signed so that you and Lady Durham can put things behind you."

Soon enough, she found out exactly what that meant.

137

More importantly, what it might mean as time went on.

Chapter Eighteen

Isaac had never been happier than when their marriage certificate was signed, and Kent's meddlesome ways were behind them. Because no matter what the blackguard did at this point, the last banns had been posted and he and Clara were, by law, officially married.

"Stay on for dinner, minister," Blake said. "We insist."

"I appreciate the invitation, my lords," he shook his head, "but we all know it best I not dally and return to town."

"And why is that, again?" Clara asked after the minister left.

"Because he is a busy man." Isaac smiled at Mabel, not wanting her to overhear his nefarious explanation when it came. He murmured as much in Clara's ear, too. For the evening's events had been a scheme indeed.

She smiled and nodded, and they continued on with their evening. First a lovely dinner, then some more piano playing, during which Mabel finally played a few notes.

"I think perhaps it's someone's bedtime," Isaac finally announced when Mabel's eyes grew heavy.

"I assure you," Mabel said on a yawn, "I am quite awake."

"I can see that." He crouched in front of her and smiled. "Nonetheless, you must get your beauty sleep."

"Beauty sleep?"

"Yes." He smiled wider still. "Have you not heard of it?"

She shook her head. "No, but I very much like the sound of it."

"Of course you would because you are beautiful. Therefore, it's sleep designed just for you." He reached into his pocket. "But first, I must give you something to officially welcome you to the family."

"Officially?" She cocked her head, a hopeful glint in her eyes. "As a father might?"

"Precisely as a father might." He urged her to hold out her wrist and clasped a bracelet around it. "Ah, yes, it looks perfect on you, Lady Mabel."

"Oh, *my*." Her eyes rounded on the ruby bracelet. "How *lovely*." She glanced at her mother. "Isn't it lovely?" Her gaze went to Clara's hand. "And it matches your ring!"

"It does." Clara smiled. "A beautiful gift, to be sure, daughter."

"Thank you." Mabel flung her arms around Isaac. "Thank you so very much, my lord."

His heart swelled. "My pleasure, Lady Mabel."

"That was a lovely gesture," Clara said after Mabel was taken up to bed by Mrs. Angus. "Truly very thoughtful."

"It was, my lord," Maude said from her perch beside Blake. She offered a curious smile. "Between the ring and bracelet, an exquisite ruby set."

"And necklace." Isaac pulled a slender box out of his cloak and handed it to Clara. "For you, my dear."

She gasped when she opened it.

"Oh, Isaac," she whispered, stunned.

A chain of smaller shimmering rubies gave way to a larger diamond-encrusted ruby cuddled at the necklace's heart.

"Allow me?" He brushed aside her hair from the back and draped it around her neck, noting the way she barely breathed and how gooseflesh rose on her flawless skin.

"It looks beautiful on you," Maude praised.

"Aye," Blake agreed, smiling.

"Thank you," she murmured to Isaac, turning her head a fraction, giving him her delicate profile.

While he had wanted her more times than he could count over the years, his desire for her at that moment was never stronger. Never so intense. In fact, it took everything not to scoop her up and steal her away right then and there. To at last bring her to his bed, *their* bed, and feel what should have been his long before now.

"So tell us how you so masterfully wove all this," Maude finally gushed, having held back longer than Isaac thought she would. "For surely, this turned out to be a grand love story that will be told for generations." Her eyes widened on Isaac when he and Clara sat together. "The tale of the marquess who saved his kingdom from the wicked madam of the night, only to give it away to save his one true love."

"Maude," Clara looked skyward, "that's a bit much, don't you think?"

"Perhaps," Blake mused, winking at Isaac. "But a love story all the same."

"Do tell." Maude looked between the men. "Share everything. For I sense a scrumptious bit of scandal here."

"Or you are just looking for one," Clara countered with amusement, eyeing Isaac. "Though I will admit to being curious, as I surmise, your grand plan began right there in the minister's office."

"It did," he confessed. "For, I realized soon enough, only one thing would free you from Kent."

"Treasure," Maude murmured, her eyes wider still. "A beautiful ruby fit for a queen but given to a monster."

"No truer words were spoken." Blake smiled at her. "A monster who had to be dealt with swiftly."

"Not on the rhetorical battlefield," she surmised, "but rather, off it."

"Correct." Blake tapped his temple. "So, it became not a battle by gun but by wit."

"And wit our lord has." Clara perked a brow at Isaac. "Wit that decided anger was not the best course of action but rather," she tilted her head in question, "mock compliance?"

"Right you are." Isaac nodded. "It made more sense to take Kent seriously than confront him then and there with a pistol."

"Because giving him the impression you believed him lent credence to your grand plan, aye, old chap?" Blake prompted.

"It did," Isaac concurred. "Best that Kent thinks I ultimately believed his document authentic even though I did not."

Maude cocked her head, putting the pieces together. "So that there could be no questioning your bargain?"

"That's right," Blake answered.

"The gem," Clara murmured, glancing at Isaac, not quite grasping it until she did. "It's not real, is it?"

"Not in the least." Isaac rested his elbow on the back of the seat beside her and trailed his fingers ever-so-slightly here and there. From her shoulder to the side of her neck to the dainty shell of her ear. A small smile ghosted his face. "It seems our fortune teller might have been onto something after all."

"With what she said to me, most certainly." She met his small smile. "For what weighed on my mind most, the unknown words that I feared, were if you still loved me as I love you."

"Which I very much do." He brushed his fingers along the nape of her neck, eager to touch more of her. To explore every little part lost to him. "As to what she said to me, it was spot on."

"Only you can determine how much she is worth when danger comes," Clara murmured, repeating the woman's words. "Remember, *that* is what it is for."

"That's right," he confirmed.

"Was I worth but a fake jewel then?" she said softly. Her cheeks pinkened when she looked at him. "For that's how one might take it."

"And they would be wrong because you are worth so much more." He tilted her chin until their gazes aligned. "I would have given Kent everything to keep you and Mabel safe. Of that, there can be no question." The corner of his mouth inched up. "Until we got to that point, though, I figured I would try the fake jewel first. A jewel that could very well be what our fortune teller referred to when she said, '*that* is what it is for.' We will never know for sure, but it suits the situation, does it not?" He smiled. "Either way, just look what I got for it. More than money could ever buy."

"Very true." Clara met his smile. "We both did."

"Well, clearly, you got far more than what Lord Kent left with." Taken by the whole thing, Maude chuckled. "A *seemingly* valuable piece considering that fellow authenticated it and all."

"Indeed." Blake chuckled. "I'd say our local actor-turned-jeweler made a jolly good show of it, too. Quite talented, to be sure." He winked at Maude. "For, in truth, Kent left with nothing more than a big, bulky albeit very pretty bauble. One that Lord Durham's great-great-grandfather made for amusement at gatherings and, as rumor has it, to substantiate his wealth to potential investors." He held up his glass to Isaac. "Congratulations to a job well done, cousin. You thought of everything."

"So it seems." Clara's gaze never left Isaac. "And the ride back? Why lead me to believe one thing when you could have just been truthful?"

"Because there was no point giving you false hope when I didn't know if the archbishop's signature was authentic, and I might lose you," he explained. "I fibbed about my late wife, and I needing a special license, so I have no idea what the bishop's signature looks like." He smiled as he wrapped one of her curls around his finger.

"That in mind, it was best that I figure out who would go along with my quickly concocted scheme first." He shook his head. "There was no way to know if the minister, magistrate, constable, and our good actor would all take part."

"Yet in such little time, they did?"

"But of course," Blake replied. "Lord Durham does so much for so many, it's no wonder they came to his aid with so little notice. He is much welcome in these parts, and I suspect they are glad to see him home and settled at last."

"No doubt they are," Maude echoed, praising Isaac. "Well done, my lord." She grinned between him and Clara. "Well done, indeed!" She narrowed an eye. "Yet one has to wonder…what happens when Lord Kent figures out he has been swindled? For surely, he will eventually."

"I strongly suspect once he does, he will keep quiet about it to avoid embarrassment," Isaac said dryly. "Not only that, but if that *is* the archbishop's signature, which I do so hope it's not, I imagine the bishop will want no further involvement and prefer the matter to go away quietly." He shrugged a shoulder. "If it *is* a forged signature, Kent will be facing another set of problems altogether. As it was, after our good minister left this evening, he sent a copy to the archbishop to assess."

"Here, here!" Blake raised his glass. "In any event, it no longer matters because Duchess Surrey is now officially Marchioness Durham. Therefore, by law, she is untouchable."

"*Well* played," Maude congratulated. "Though…" She put a hand to her heart and whipped out her fan. "I will admit the adventurer, and perhaps even the romantic in me, mourns the loss of a genuine family treasure. To think it never truly existed is a bit of a shame, is it not?"

"Was such said then?" Isaac murmured, kissing Clara's hand near her ring. "Or was it assumed?"

It took no time to figure out his implication.

"Heavens be, *no!*" Maude's eyes widened on Clara's ring. "Is *that...*" her gaze rose to the necklace, "and *it?*" Her gaze rounded further still. "And Lady Mabel's bracelet?"

Blake raised his glass to Isaac again. "Well done, indeed!"

He raised his glass in return, not answering Maude's question but then there was no need. The family jewel, now broken down into several gems, had, in fact, remained with his kin for hundreds of years despite MacLauchlin Castle being rebuilt several times and pirates becoming part of the fold. But then he supposed it was those very ancestors he could thank for his devious scheming, no matter how well-intended.

The night wore on, the evening everything he imagined his and Clara's wedding night might be. Not some crowded grand affair but shared with a few close friends. Good food and excellent music followed by conversations he could enjoy with her rather than feel the need to separate himself from.

"What changed your mind?" Clara asked at one point. "When did you decide to take a chance on a new family?"

"When you reminded me that I had not lost everyone I cared about," he replied. "When you reminded me Blake was still here. Mabel and you." He traced the curvature of her cheek, saying words he never imagined he would. "So very much you, my love, for you hold my heart. You always have."

Something he at long last showed her when he took her up to bed.

When he finally did what he had given up hope he might ever do again.

Chapter Nineteen

Clara had thought perhaps when Isaac finally brought her up to bed that he would want to talk more, as they were once again chatting like they used to, but he did no such thing. Instead, he set her down, cupped her cheeks, and kissed her with so much passion it made her weep.

"Isaac," she murmured against his lips, swept away by how he made her feel. Wanting so much more. "Please."

Just as eager, he tore off his jacket and yanked at his cravat as he gently lowered first one shoulder of her dress, then the other, seeming to cherish the act. Desire built in his steady gaze, and for several long moments, he simply looked at her. Took her in as though savoring the moment. As though envisioning what was beneath her corset and chemise, though the final unveiling was but moments away.

Or so she thought until he reeled her against him and kissed her more passionately still. All the while, he stroked and caressed her, taking his time, enjoying her body, building her pleasure. His talented fingers explored, dusting lightly here and there, sending delicious sensations through her before he cupped the side of her neck with one hand and worked the laces on her corset with the other.

Shivers of arousal shot through her when he peppered kisses down her neck and inhaled deeply as though pulling in her scent. As though enjoying her in the most primal way. He tossed aside her corset and continued touching her, building her passion with every caress. Tempting her with what was to come. How he intended to make her feel.

By the time he dropped to his knees, gazed up at her with worship, and gently pulled her chemise down, exposing bit by bit her pale flesh, she felt near-liquefied. So aroused, her legs barely held her up. The way he looked at her was almost as erotic as the feel of the material sliding down her prone body.

Her nipples pebbled, and her breathing quickened as she stood nude in front of him. As she offered herself up. His hungry eyes never left her face as he tossed aside his cravat then tore off his shirt. Then, seeming to visually devour her every step of the way, his gaze began a slow, sensual wander down her torso.

"Bloody hell, you are glorious," he groaned, at last touching her bare flesh, trailing his fingers in the wake of his eyes. Adoring her as only he could, outdoing her fantasies of this moment when he fondled her breasts, then pulled a taut nipple into his mouth.

She cried out, and her legs grew even weaker, but he held her up, dropping soft kisses down her belly until he made his way to the juncture between her thighs. He inhaled deeply, groaning in approval before he grasped her backside and flicked his tongue over the tiny nub at the apex of her pleasure.

"Isaac," she moaned. When her legs gave out altogether, she was glad he laid her on the plush carpet in front of the fire rather than carry her to bed.

She needed him now.

Here.

Nowhere else.

"Undress," she pleaded when he spread her legs and licked the overly sensitive flesh between her thighs again. "I want to see all of you," she barely managed to whisper when he kissed and licked, again and again, seeming to lose himself in the taste of her.

She, in turn, lost herself in the pleasure spiraling through her.

"Husband," she gasped, struggling to breathe, clenching the carpet when he suckled her sweet spot more aggressively.

"Wife," he breathed against her tender folds, his breath like molten fire.

His lips might have shown her mercy as he kissed his way back up her body, but his fingers held her prisoner when he continued working her eager, swollen flesh. When he slid first one, then two fingers into her, she thought she would come undone.

"Oh, God," she panted against his lips before he kissed her more deeply, then pulled back and watched her. Watched as he stroked and loved her with his fingers. As he drew her closer and closer until she flew over the edge.

She trembled, trying to hold onto him, trying to stay with him, but her body had a mind of its own, and he vanished. Or so she thought until he was there again in all his glory.

"My love," she whispered, grateful when his lips returned to hers. When he kissed her with a passion she would never tire of.

"Yes, Clara," he whispered before meeting her eyes again. Before showing her in one look that he was here, not somewhere else in his mind. Not hiding from what might happen between them. "I'm here."

That's all he needed to say.

Feel.

Be.

The sensation of him filling her, being inside her, was almost more than she could bear—more than she could have imagined. Whimpering with pleasure, reminding him she was long past being a virgin, she urged him on when he hesitated.

She wanted all he could offer.

148

All they could become.

He braced himself on an elbow, and their gazes connected as he cupped her cheek with his free hand, and moved, thrusting so well, so deeply, that everything inside her came alive.

Every nerve ending.

Every bit of long-dormant flesh.

His eyes stayed with hers until, eventually, his features contorted in bliss, and he moved faster. She clenched his shoulders and wrapped her legs around him, wanting him closer.

Deeper.

Part of her.

Sweat slicked their skin as frenzied passion only intensified. Flared out of control.

"Hell," he gasped, thrusting harder still, rolling his hips, hitting every last bit of throbbing flesh, giving her what she needed.

But then, based on the tortured pleasure on his face, he felt the same.

Needed the same.

"I cannot," he growled, fighting it even as he embraced it. "You feel too good…"

That's all it took to catapult her over the edge. Untouchable sensation screamed through her. She arched and cried out as he released a strangled groan, pressed deep one last time, shuddered, and pulsed inside her.

Little was said after that as they drifted down from the great heights they had taken each other. But then what was there to say? They knew how they felt, what they wanted. And it was only ever each other. So said the way they luxuriated in each other's arms before he carried her to bed and made love to her again.

And again.

Over and over.

In fact, they loved each other so often and so well that the future turned out bright indeed, and whatever curse Isaac thought had fallen on him lifted. So said the son who came the following year, then the daughter after that.

But not before Lord Kent was eventually arrested for forgery and his fake gem confiscated.

On an even happier note, Maude eventually became Lady MacLauchlin and mistress of her very own Scottish castle, where her chatty ways reportedly kept all well-entertained.

As generations to come would often say, Isaac and Clara's was a tale of saving each other. Of rediscovering great love in a most unusual way. Some said Isaac MacLauchlin, Marquess of Durham, was tamed by the woman who nefariously forced him into marriage, but his family knew better. She had simply led him back to the man he once was. A truly happy one for the rest of his days.

Author's Note

Interested in traveling back to the medieval period and following the MacLauchlins in Isaac's paintings? Join Laird Keenan MacLauchlin and his brothers in Sky's *Highlander's Pact* series and Isaac's pirate ancestors in her *Pirates of Britannia* stories, *The Seafaring Rogue,* and its sequel, *The Sea Hellion.*

About the Author

Sky Purington is the bestselling author of over fifty novels and novellas. A New Englander born and bred who recently moved to Virginia, Purington married her hero, has an amazing son who inspires her daily, and two ultra-lovable husky shepherd mixes. Passionate for variety, Sky's vivid imagination spans several romance genres, including historical, time travel, paranormal, and fantasy. Expect steamy stories teeming with protective alpha heroes and strong-minded heroines.

Purington loves to hear from readers and can be contacted at Sky@SkyPurington.com. Interested in keeping up with Sky's latest news and releases? Either visit Sky's website, www.SkyPurington.com, join her quarterly newsletter, or sign up for personalized text message alerts. Simply text 'skypurington' (no quotes, one word, all lowercase) to 74121 or visit Sky's Sign-up Page. Texts will ONLY be sent when there is a new book release. Readers can easily opt out at any time.

Made in the USA
Monee, IL
11 May 2021